PRAISE F

"As action packed as a Tom Clancy thriller... narrowing... adrenaline-laced."

—Michiko Kakutani, *New York Times*

"Pulses with the grit of a Jerry Bruckheimer production..."

—*Washington Post*

"Reveals an intimate look at the rigorous training and perilous missions of the best of the Navy's best."

—*Time*

"Well written... an exciting book."

—*Seattle Post-Intelligencer*

"Cuts straight to the chase. The literary equivalent of a Hollywood blockbuster... compelling and inspiring."

—*Miami Herald*

"A rare glimpse into the thinking, training, and tactics of the Special Forces at a time when their shadowy work is playing an increasingly crucial role in the war on terror."

—*San Diego Union-Tribune*

"Another great novel reflecting our spec ops forces' global capabilities. Written by a proven and insightful master storyteller."

—Howard E. Wasdin, former SEAL Team Six sniper and *NYT* best-selling author of *SEAL Team Six: Memoirs of an Elite Navy SEAL Sniper*

"A masterful blend... not knowing if you're about to take a bullet to the head from a SEAL sniper or get hit in the gut with a punch line."

—Dalton Fury, former Delta Force commander and *NYT* best-selling author of *Kill Bin Laden*

"Grabs you on page one and is hard to put down."

—General Henry H. Shelton, former commander in chief of the US Special Operations Command and 14th chairman of the Joint Chiefs of Staff

"A must read."

—Jack Coughlin, former gunnery sergeant, USMC, and best-selling author of *Shooter*

"A muscular thrill ride that's rich with detail and full of heart and energy. A standout in the ranks of modern action-adventure thrillers."

—Mark Greaney, #1 *NYT* best-selling coauthor of *Command Authority*, by Tom Clancy with Mark Greaney

"Eloquent, realistic, humorous, and thought-provoking..."

—Mark Beder, former lieutenant commander, SEAL assault team leader

ALSO BY STEPHEN TEMPLIN

Special Operations Group Thrillers

Trident's First Gleaming[#1] Chris, Hannah, & Sonny

From Russia without Love[#2] Chris, Hannah, & Sonny

Autumn Assassins [#3] Max & Tom

Assassin's Sons [#4] Max & Tom

Patriot Dream[#5] Chris, Hannah, Sonny, Max, & Tom

Special Operations Group Short Story

Dead in Damascus[#0] Chris & Hannah

Sonny Spy Down[#1] Sonny

Nonfiction

Navy SEAL Training Class 144: My BUD/S Journal

SEAL Team Six: Memoirs of an Elite Navy SEAL Sniper

I Am a SEAL Team Six Warrior (Young Adult version of *SEAL Team Six*)

SEAL Team Six Outcast Novels

SEAL Team Six: Outcasts[#1]

Easy Day for the Dead[#2]

Patriot Dream
[#5] A Special Operations Group Thriller
Stephen Templin

Friends... they cherish one another's hopes. They are kind to one another's dreams.

–Henry David Thoreau
Philosopher

Chapter One

Five covert CIA operators—two of them dead men walking—stepped off a Pershing 62 muscle yacht docked in the Mediterranean. An orange ball of morning light rose above the heart of Rome, about thirty klicks away, increasing the motion of ships on the sea and planes over Leonardo Da Vinci International Airport in the distance. The higher the summer sun climbed, the hotter Rome became.

Chris Paladin felt uneasy as he took a seat in the back of a gray Fiat Freemont, a midsize SUV parked on the pier. Max Wayne was one of the dead men walking, but he maintained his devil-may-care posture as he rode shotgun. Tom Wayne was Max's younger brother and the other dead man walking. He got behind the wheel, put the SUV in drive, and used the GPS on his phone to navigate.

Tom steered away from the sea. The municipality of Rome spread across almost five hundred square miles, including the airport, outlying farms, the famous downtown area, and more. Tom weaved through Ostia, a subdivision on the southwest edge of the city. Behind a row of buildings, trash bins overflowed with garbage. Farther ahead, the streets became clean, and Tom rolled along Tancredi Chiaraluce Street beside the yellowish Tiber River. He continued for a klick and a half past small boats and yachts moored in the river and sitting on dry land.

Max and Tom were infected with a deadly virus called BK-16, a new assassination bioweapon developed by the Russians—and they only had one day to live. Their five-member team had to snatch the antidote from a Russian lab thirty-two klicks away. If they failed, there'd be no coming back from the dead for Max and Tom.

Beside Chris sat his best friend, Hannah Andrade, whom CIA had tapped to be their team leader. She was still recovering from a severe concussion. Chris's stomach twisted. *She should've taken more time to recover.* But there was no time to worry—he had to focus on the mission. They all did.

"Can't you go faster?" Max asked. "We have to reach the lab before the FSB does." FSB was short for *Fedral'naya Sluzhba Bezopasnosh*—Russia's spy agency.

Sonny Cohen gave Tom some of his Queens, New York, attitude: "You drive like old people hump." Sonny was an experienced operator "on loan" to CIA from the Army's Delta Force. He'd worked with Chris and Hannah on two missions and with Max and Tom on one, but this was his first time operating with all four operators at the same time.

"You two whining about his driving isn't going to get us there faster," Chris said.

The street split away from the river and rolled past undeveloped countryside and farmland before entering the burbs.

Hannah read something on her cell phone. "Uh-oh."

"What?" Chris asked.

She tapped her phone. "Langley wants us to destroy the lab, too."

"As if we didn't have enough to do," Sonny said.

"Now they tell us," Max said.

She turned to Chris and asked, "What do you think?"

Chris pondered for a moment. "If there's a chance to destroy the lab, sure. If not, oh well. Getting that antidote is number one."

"You guys hear that?" Hannah asked.

"Yes," Tom said.

Max nodded. "Yep."

Sonny grunted.

Seeing Hannah check her cell phone reminded Chris to see if his battery was charged. It was. He also wanted to verify that a secret app CIA had installed on his phone was functional. He typed a code into his search bar, 4 Nikkia, using the name of his elementary school friend.

A secure screen of apps appeared, and he opened the car hacking app, developed by Langley. If this mission went south, he could use his phone to "borrow" a car to escape and evade capture. Using his smartphone, he could access most vehicles through their remote key systems, vehicle locators, remote engine starters, Bluetooth, radio, cellular, or WiFi. Most automakers bought equipment from the same small number of suppliers using the same small number of frequencies. Once those frequencies were hacked, the door to their operating systems opened wide. Automobile security was more than a decade behind in closing those doors, and the car industry didn't have an effective business model or incentive to catch up. Satisfied that the app was operational, he closed it.

Outside the SUV, buildings became taller, more numerous, and packed closer together as Chris and his teammates entered the heart of Rome. On the right appeared the red brick remains of ancient public baths, covering a hundred thousand square meters of land and standing thirteen stories tall.

"We're a klick away from the lab," Tom said.

With five people in the SUV the interior had become uncomfortably warm, but they were near their target so Chris didn't complain.

"What, is the A/C broken?" Sonny asked.

Max put the cooler on high.

"About damn time," Sonny said.

The deeper they traveled into the heart of Rome, the less the rules of the road seemed to matter. A Roman in an orange Lamborghini thundered between lanes and ran a red stoplight, but in this thick traffic, Tom couldn't drive faster than thirty miles per hour. Other drivers missed the Lamborghini in a sort of organized chaos. The Lambo disappeared like part of a dream.

They passed the remains of a palace, temples, and other ancient buildings resting on a lush, green hill to the left. Then came the Arch of Constantine, standing two stories high, one epic archway flanked by two smaller ones. In spite of its height, the arch was dwarfed in the shadow of the Colosseum—over thirty times taller.

The Colosseum reminded Chris of the 2000 film *Gladiator*, and he experienced the anxiety of General Maximus Meridius, waiting for the gate to the arena to open—waiting to do battle. Chris wanted to touch the sound-suppressed FN P90 personal defense weapon in the swing-out shoulder holster concealed under his suit jacket. He thought the physical contact with it might provide reassurance and deliver him from his anxiety, but he knew it was a bad habit to get into. Maybe not now, but sometime in the future, an enemy could notice him touching his concealed weapon and his cover could be blown. Chris resisted the impulse to handle it.

The others also carried the futuristic-looking weapon with its polymer rectangular design and two odd curvy holes in the bottom of it. The unusual Belgian configuration gave the FN P90 major league muzzle velocity, accuracy, maneuverability, and ergonomics in a light, concealable package—excellent for "low-visibility" ops such as this. At twenty inches in length and weighing less than six pounds, it was larger than a pistol but smaller than an assault rifle. Chris simply liked it because it was reliable, quiet, and lethal.

He took a deep breath and exhaled long and hard. He recited one of General Maximus Meridius's lines: "Brothers, what we do in life echoes in eternity."

Max quoted *Gladiator*, too: "At my signal, unleash hell."

"This is Sparta!" Sonny shouted.

"Wrong movie, King Leo," Hannah said.

Sonny shrugged his shoulders.

Tom kept his eyes on the road. "In both those movies, the heroes died."

"Thanks, buzzkill," Max said.

Sonny spoke loudly: "Live fast, die young, and leave a classy corpse."

Hannah pursed her lips. "Nobody's going to die."

Under the opposite side of Chris's shoulder holster, he carried two extra fifty-round magazines of FN 5.7 x 28mm ammo. On his belt, he carried two flash-bangs and one smoke grenade, each of French origin—nothing they carried could be traced to the US.

Tom hung a right and passed a touristy section of hotels and restaurants. "How many FSB officers did the scientist say were in the lab?"

"Ten," Max said.

Sonny snorted. "She didn't know."

Under Chris's shirt was a mic that transmitted speech vibrations from his throat: "Radio check." In his ear was a receiver the size of a pea that was magnetized for easy retrieval later.

"Yeah," Max said.

"Sounds good," Hannah said.

"Loud and clear," Tom said.

"I'll have two soft tacos, a bean burrito, and a Coke," Sonny said.

Hannah rolled her eyes and Chris and Max chuckled.

Tom pulled into an alley between two rows of buildings. A dozen cars were parked behind the structures. Finding a parking spot in Rome in midday should've been difficult, but Hannah had arranged for an asset to hold a spot for them with his silver-colored Citroen C3. It was parked two buildings away from the lab. As soon as Tom neared it, the Citroen pulled out, and Tom steered the SUV into the space.

"Wish we could do this at night," Chris muttered, "under the cover of darkness."

"Time is ticking," Hannah said. "We have to snatch the antidote before Minotaur does." She used the codename of the FSB officer who a defected scientist said was coming to pick up vials of BK-16 and its antidote.

Tom stayed behind the wheel with the engine running while Chris and the others exited. Hannah carried an empty satchel to pack the antidote in. The foursome converged on the back of a sand-colored four-story building—the lab—and climbed its metal stairs. The stairs were an unadorned back exit, sturdier than a fire escape. The defected scientist had given them details of the building, inside and out; the location of the antidote; and keys.

On the third floor, they "stacked up," taking positions on both sides of the door—weapons ready. Chris lined up first to enter. He'd done numerous building entries, and each time he expected the unexpected. Much of the time, his expectations were fulfilled. Chris took a deep breath.

Hannah produced the key from her pocket, unlocked the door and pushed it open.

Chris slipped inside as point man. The hallway extended left and right. He aimed left and advanced. In a corner was a potted plant that smelled of mint. The hallway turned ninety degrees, then turned again.

Now he was in a long corridor with a blond man standing at the other end. The man turned around. Chris shuffled forward and motioned for him to freeze. But the man reached for something on his hip and drew it—a pistol. Chris maintained his forward progress and shot him twice in the chest. The shots made less noise than the quiet clicking of the P90's parts: *tick-tick*.

"Agghh," the man grunted.

Chris silenced him with a shot to the skull. Blood splattered, and he dropped like an anchor.

"Who is it?" a male voice asked in Russian from somewhere in the building.

Chris stepped over the body and blood spatter. Then he rounded the next turn. The hall had taken him in a crooked S shape. There was a door to his right. Chris and the others stacked up.

Once again, Hannah unlocked the door. This time, she threw it open.

Chris stepped into a break room where five armed men were standing. Or at least, Chris thought it was five men—there was no time to count. A bald thuggish guy in the northeast corner aimed a pistol in Chris's direction, but Chris gunned him down and pressed deeper into the room. *Keep advancing... don't jam up everyone behind you.*

In his peripheral vision, Chris saw Max peel off to the opposite corner, and Sonny dissected the middle of the room. More sound-suppressed shots were fired—*tick, tick, tick*—but Chris was too focused on his area of responsibility to see which of his teammates was shooting or who or what they were shooting at.

A door opened from somewhere, but Chris couldn't distinguish whether the sound came from inside the room or an adjacent room. He posted in the northwest corner and guarded the break room. Although he thought he'd seen five enemies in the space, now there were only four bad guys sprawled out bleeding on the deck. Maybe he'd counted wrong. Or one had escaped.

Sonny stood rough and ready in another corner. Max was in his spot, too. Now they commanded the whole room and its six doors.

Hannah inserted a key into the doorknob of one of the two storage rooms on the west wall—where the scientist said the BK-16 and its antidote was stored.

In the middle of the room were white plastic chairs neatly wrapped around four wooden tables, and against one wall was a gas stove next to a kitchen counter with a microwave, paper towels, sugar, olive oil, and other kitchen items. One of the doors on the east wall opened. From Chris's angle he couldn't see through the doorway, but Max had a better view, and he shot multiple times into the room beyond.

Then a door near the northeast corner opened, and a party-crasher burst through, waving his pistol like he was about to go postal. Both Chris and Sonny got the drop on him. Chris rapidly pulled the trigger and stitched the party-crasher's arm to his side, and Sonny embroidered his front. Chris finished him off with a pop to the side of the skull. Party-crasher's upper body maintained momentum into the room, but his feet seemed glued to the deck, and he did a face-plant.

Party-crasher's open door gave Chris a slice of a view into the next room, but he couldn't see the whole room, and he couldn't leave his teammates to investigate. Sonny had a fuller picture from his angle—he fired through the doorway.

Three shots rang out. They weren't sound-suppressed, and Chris couldn't process where they came from—things happened too rapidly.

Hannah was still inside the storage room. Chris hoped she was okay, but she was a big girl, and he didn't flood the radio with useless chatter.

Chris spotted a fifth body on the floor of the room he was in. He'd lost sight of it earlier because it had fallen beneath some tables that obscured his vision.

From Party-crasher's open door, a man wearing a white smock appeared. Chris aimed and wondered why Sonny hadn't picked him off first, and then he realized why—the man wasn't armed. White Smock looked Italian, said something in Italian, and raised his hands. Chris motioned anxiously for him to get down on the deck, but the man froze in shock.

Max aimed as if he was going to shoot Sonny, but he shot through the doorway and out into the hall their team had come in from earlier. A thud sounded, like a body hitting the floor. Sonny must've heard the rounds whip past him because his eyes opened wide.

"I have the package," Hannah said. "Coming out." She radioed the message so the good guys wouldn't mistake her for a bad guy. She stepped out, her satchel bulging, and turned. A door near her opened, outside of Chris and Max's direct fields of fire. Hannah didn't have eyes in the back of her head to see who was behind her. Sonny appeared to have a clear shot, but Hannah's body blocked part of it. If he fired, he might hit her. If he didn't fire, whoever opened the door might kill her. Or maybe the person in the doorway was another unarmed civilian—only Sonny could see for sure. Sonny fired: *Tick-tick. Tick.* Then it sounded as if someone had dropped a sack of potatoes. *Another one bites the dust.*

Sonny's rounds had ripped danger-close to Hannah. She paused and seemed startled for a moment. Then she resumed her shuffle, P90 aimed in front of her. "I'll take us out."

Max gazed at the stove for a moment before he approached it and turned the knobs on high without engaging the flame. *Hsssss.*

"What're you doing?" Chris asked.

Max took the cap off the bottle of olive oil, dumped it on the paper towels, pulled out a Bic lighter, and lit the paper towels. The fire licked the wood cabinet above. "Exactly what it looks like, padre." The gleam of a pyromaniac flashed in his eyes.

Hannah departed the room, and Chris hastened out behind her. He stepped over a corpse in the hall, then another.

Hannah proceeded through the crooked S-shaped hall.

Footsteps sounded behind.

Chapter Two

Chris turned around to see the source of the footsteps—Sonny and Max. Then Chris returned his eyes to the front, scanning for threats.

Hannah rounded the corner. Chris followed her. The minty odor returned, but now the hall smelled of olive oil past its smoke point—like burning rubber. An alarm from the building went off. If it was a security alarm, it was oddly late. More likely, it was a fire alarm.

Max sounded thoroughly amused on the radio: "Lab is on fire—might explode."

"Did you...?" Hannah asked.

"Yeah," Max said proudly.

Hannah's voice was ecstatic: "Bad to the bone." Wind beneath her wings, she picked up the pace and exited the building. Descending the exterior steps down to the alley, she glanced back and smiled. Chris grinned. *We have the antidote, the lab is on fire, and none of us were injured.* The sunshine and a light breeze tickled his skin.

Chris glanced at the stairs above to see if Sonny and Max were still with them. They were. Below him, Hannah stepped off the stairs and into the alley.

"Gray Mercedes van entered the alley," Tom said over the radio.

Chris didn't know whether Minotaur and his FSB buddies were in the van or if this would be some random civilian. He couldn't see the van, but that was okay, because whoever was in it couldn't see him, either. The closest place to hide was between a white box truck and a red Audi Q2, a compact SUV. Hannah took cover between the two vehicles, and Chris joined her. Sonny and Max descended the final steps and took refuge with them. The white truck shielded them from the gray van's view.

"Tomahawk, we need an extract," Max said over the radio, using Tom's call sign.

"Gray van is between you and me—blocking the alley," Tom said.

"Can you see who's inside?" Sonny asked.

"Windows are black," Tom replied. "Van is just sitting there with the engine idling."

"What are they waiting for?" Hannah asked.

"Us," Sonny said.

"We don't know that," Max said.

Chris took out his phone and opened his car hacking app. On the menu, it gave a list of car makes; he scrolled through them and selected Audi. The menu prompted him to select the location—he scrolled to Europe and selected it. Then the app prompted him to choose the car brand. He pressed Q2. The screen read: Waiting to communicate.

"Smoke leaking out of the third floor," Tom said over the radio.

The fire alarm blared incessantly.

"We can't go back in there," Sonny said.

"We can't sit here, either," Max said.

Hannah's voice became tense: "Cops and others will be here any moment."

On Chris's cell phone, two options showed: Unlock door and Start engine. He tapped the first. The red Audi's doors clicked.

"What the...?" Sonny said.

Chris opened the car's door and seated himself behind the wheel. "Get in."

Sonny rode shotgun, and Max and Hannah hopped in back.

Chris locked the doors and pressed Start engine on his phone. The engine didn't start.

Tom's voice became anxious: "Three dudes with assault rifles and a fourth with a short shotgun exiting the van. One of the guys with an assault rifle has gray hair and wears a gray suit."

"Minotaur and his crew," Chris guessed aloud. He pressed the ignition button on the car. Nothing.

Sonny pounded the dash once. "Come on, you goombah piece of crap!"

Max shook Chris's seat from behind, throttling him. "Go, go, go!" Chris pressed the ignition button on the car again. This time, the engine rumbled. "Yes!"

"Two more guys with assault rifles exited the van!" Tom exclaimed. "All six are heading your way—you have to get out of there!"

Chris looked behind and backed out of the parking space, the rear end of the vehicle facing in the direction of the gunmen and their van. He stomped on the accelerator. Adrenaline blasted through his body, and the world seemed to slow. *Need more speed.* He crushed the accelerator to the deck. The car still didn't seem to go fast enough. A half dozen armed guys came into view. They split ranks and scattered, but the smallest of them was too slow, and Chris struck him. Shorty separated from his rifle and catapulted backwards before he bounced off the van.

Chris stomped on the brake, and the wheels screeched to a halt. He shifted into drive and peeled out. His wheels squealed and smoked like a creature escaping Hell.

Suddenly it sounded as if Fourth of July fireworks had begun. Chris and Sonny ducked. *Pshh, pshh* went the rear window. Sparkling particles of glass sprayed the inside of the Audi. Rounds cracked past Chris's ear. Two holes popped through the middle of the front windshield, and another smacked the windshield in front of where Chris's head had been.

"There's a bullet hole in your headrest, Reverend," Max said, using Chris's call sign.

"Are you okay?" Hannah asked.

"No injuries," Chris said.

"Good that you ducked," Sonny said.

The Audi's engine whined, and Chris only stuck his head up high enough to see over the dash as he barreled through the alley.

The shooting stopped, and Chris sat up straight and glanced in his rearview mirror. "Anyone hit?"

The rear window was busted. In the distance behind them, the shooters scrambled into their van.

In front of Chris, a worker unloaded packages from a truck. Chris didn't want to take an innocent life. He swerved. *Miss.* The Audi dropped into a dip and Chris felt heavy for a moment until the SUV blew up out of the dip, and he experienced weightlessness. His breathing became rapid, and his heart beat fortissimo.

Parked cars and the backs of buildings cruised by. A subcompact car started to back out of a space, but Chris laid on the horn without stopping. The car braked, and Chris avoided hitting it by only a few inches. A pedestrian began to walk across the alley, but jumped back out of the way. A group of pigeons took flight from the pavement, but one didn't fly fast enough and bounced off the windshield, leaving a spot of feathers and blood on the glass.

At the end of the alley, Chris turned left. A hubcap popped off and rolled into the street. He passed restaurants and shops. "I'll head north until our tail is clean. Then I'll circle around and return to the yacht."

"Anywhere is better than here," Sonny said.

Chris could see part of the Colosseum up ahead. Elsewhere in the city, sirens squealed. He made a right on Piazza del Colosseo.

In the rearview mirror, the van turned onto the road behind them.

Chris wanted to follow the road counterclockwise around the Colosseum, but it was a one-way street going against him, and a sign with a red circle and horizontal bar in the middle warned him to keep out. Even so, traffic wasn't quite bumper-to-bumper, and Chris said, "I'm turning."

"Coola boola," Sonny cheered.

Chris steered head-on into traffic. A little blue Fiat Panda honked. It was to the right, so Chris jerked the steering wheel left. More drivers honked. A red Maserati Levante, a midsize luxury SUV, came at him from the left, so Chris swung right. Other vehicles ahead stopped, clogging the lanes.

"Are you crazy?" Max asked.

A Roman gestured with the sign of a bull with two horns and hollered, "*Cornuto!*"

"Get the hell out of there!" Sonny shouted back at the Roman.

"Make a hole!" Max hollered at the oncoming drivers.

One man shouted. "*Ti faccio un culo cosi!*" Chris recognized the word *culo* from Spanish, meaning "ass," and he didn't need to understand the rest to get the message.

In a narrow lane to the right, words written on the street seemed to indicate something about buses and taxis, as if the lane was reserved for them, and it was open, so Chris took it. More Romans threw wild gestures, shouted, and honked.

Chris passed the Colosseum, and the street became two-way again. Sonny looked into his side-view mirror. "I think we lost them."

"We did it!" Max said.

"I hate to bear bad news," Hannah said.

Chris checked his rearview mirror—the van was there.

"Damn!" Chris cursed.

"I thought you guys weren't supposed to swear," Max said.

Chris had left SEAL Team Six to become a full-time pastor. He had only accepted this mission part-time as a favor to Hannah. Chris stepped down harder on the gas. "One of my many ministerial failings." He sped past basilicas and temples colored in shades of brown and gray.

Tom's voice came over the radio, using his brother's call sign: "Yukon, Tomahawk. What's your twenty?"

Hannah pressed her muzzle against the bullet-riddled back window and fired: *tick-tick-tick-tick-tick*.

Max slung lead downrange, too. "We're on Piazza del Colosseo. Now it's Fori Imperiali Street."

Assault rifles rattled, and the rear window imploded again.

Chris whipped the wheel so savagely to the right that he almost ran off the road and hit one of the trees on the corner of Via Cavour.

Max's voice became frantic. "Hannah!"

Sonny turned around and Chris glanced in the rearview mirror. Hannah had collapsed.

"Hannah!" Chris cried out.

But there was no response.

Max touched her neck where there should have been a pulse. He shook his head.

"Hannah wake up!" Chris shouted.

"She's dead," Max said. "Hannah is dead."

Chapter Three

One week earlier...

O In a small two-man police station outside of Istanbul, a captured Russian spy, codename Minotaur, sat naked and unafraid. Some called him Shark, and others called him Devil, but his real name was Kirill Smirnov. He had the tanned skin of his Mongolian mother and the round, gray eyes and big body of his Slavic father. Minotaur's hair had gone gray in his twenties, making him appear fashionably older. He was born an old soul, and now in his thirties, he seemed wise for his age.

He knew the likelihood of capture was high, so he'd prepared accordingly. Although his pistol and other possessions had been removed when he was strip-searched, the Turkish police hadn't discovered the passive GPS transmitter hidden under a fake bloody wound and bandage on his arm. Nor did they detect the button compass, money, lock pick tools, and small improvised weapon concealed inside an aluminum cigar tube in his rectum.

Minotaur was a Spetsnaz commando who conducted assassinations, sabotage, and other covert actions deep in enemy territory for Vympel, meaning Pennant, the Russian nickname for Special Group "V." Vympel answered directly to FSB headquarters in Moscow.

Handcuffed and alone, his room was furnished only with the chair he sat on and one other. Soon the two law enforcement officers would return.

Quietly he squatted beside the chair and strained to defecate, but instead of human waste, he pushed out the cigar tube. The coating of olive oil he'd applied earlier made the process considerably easier, and now he felt relieved of the inconvenient container. It was challenging to manipulate the oily cigar container with his hands behind his back, but he'd practiced this many times, and he was an expert at it. He removed the cap from the tube and tipped out the lock pick. Then he simply inserted the pick into the lock of one cuff, turned, and it unlocked. He opened the other.

Next, he assembled his weapon: he removed the nail and pushed it through a predrilled hole in the cap. Then he replaced the cap, sandwiching the head of the nail snugly between the lid and a wooden dowel inside the tube that extended its full length. The cigar tube served as his handle and the nail protruding from the lid as the blade of his mini dagger.

Footsteps clicked in the hall. Minotaur held his hands behind his back, grasping his weapon. Two police officers, one in his thirties and the other in his twenties, entered the room. The older one looked hard around the gut, and his pistol hung tightly at an angle as if he practiced with it. The younger guy looked stronger, but his awkward posture and loose-fitting holster suggested he was inexperienced with close-quarter combat. Both wore the uniforms of Turkey's Gendarmerie—dark green trousers and light green shirts. Each gendarme carried a Yavuz 16 pistol, the Turkish version of the Beretta 92F. These country cops had a more militaristic, both-barrels-blazing reputation than their city cousins.

A cell tone rang from the senior officer's pocket, but he ignored it. He sat down and asked something in Turkish.

Minotaur spoke several languages, but he used English as his lingua franca: "I do not speak Turkish."

The senior officer's phone stopped ringing, and he asked condescendingly in English, "The gun we found on you—where did you get it?"

"From the getting place," Minotaur said.

Senior smiled with his mouth, but his eyes didn't seem happy. "Where is this *getting place?*"

"Do you have a need to know?" Minotaur asked.

"Yes, I am a police officer. Now we can do this the easy way or the hard way—it's up to you."

The junior gendarme fidgeted nervously.

Minotaur leaned toward Senior. "I recognized you before you brought me in here. You arrested a Russian diplomat, and later he died under your questioning."

"He was a spy," Senior said.

"Spy or diplomat, it matters not—what matters is that you killed him."

"Are you a spy, too?"

Minotaur stared through him. "In a remote corner of the earth, there rose from the dirt a village of warriors who couldn't be conquered. They were the fiercest warriors in the history of the world. Soon a hurricane came and wiped them out. When the waters receded, and the lands dried, all that was left of the village was dust. In the end, we all become dust."

Both Senior and Junior gave Minotaur perplexed looks.

"Why are you here?" Senior asked.

"To deliver a message."

Senior's phone rang again. This time, he pulled it out and looked at the display as if to see who the persistent caller was.

Now was Minotaur's chance. Senior appeared to be the more dangerous of the two. Minotaur leaped at him like a top fuel dragster off the starting line. Senior looked up from his phone and lifted his empty hand in self-defense. Minotaur swept Senior's defensive hand away and violently stabbed his pick into the man's temple, cracking through bone to brain with a burst of blood. Senior collapsed, and his phone bounced off the linoleum floor.

Junior reeled back on his heels and looked down at his pistol, grasping at it. "Eeee!"

Seeing the green gendarme off balance injected adrenaline into Minotaur's system like nitromethane. It felt as if he'd gone from zero to a hundred in less than a second with several g's of force pressing against him.

Junior drew his gun, but Minotaur smashed into him, and they both crashed to the floor. Junior's pistol fired, and Minotaur pounded his nail into Junior's heart. The young gendarme stopped moving, and on his shirt where he'd been struck, a dark wet spot spread slowly. Minotaur took the young man's pistol and stood. On the way to the door, Minotaur stepped over the puddle of blood forming around Senior's head.

In the office area, he found his clothes, put them on, and gathered his other belongings. He dumped the Turkish weapon in the trash and holstered his personal pistol, a Glock 19. Finally, he exited the small, two-man police station.

"Message delivered."

Chapter Four

The noon sun pummeled the color out of Istanbul as Chris sped to the edge of the city in his black Porsche Panamera, courtesy of CIA. Able to go from zero to a hundred kilometers per hour in three and a half seconds, the car was a handful, and Chris had to be careful not to draw unwanted attention from the police. The attention he wanted was from the man he was about to recruit.

Chris passed a row of multistoried concrete buildings, some faded, some new, and all adorned with signs written in Turkish. Between the buildings sat empty plots of land overgrown with weeds. He pulled up to the Mescid-i Selam Station on the Tram Four Line. His partner, Hannah, stood waiting for the tram, dressed to impress in a dress suit that was business-like, yet curvy enough to capture a man's interest.

Omer Ozturk, nicknamed Ozzie, a geeky, chubby, twenty-something man, talked with Hannah. He was the telecommunications guru for the Brotherhood of Ali, a militant Alawite Muslim organization that earned its money through smuggling illegal aliens, committing extortion, and trafficking drugs. In their spare time, they did bombings and assassinations. They supported the dictator of neighboring Syria, President Bashar al-Assad, also an Alawite Muslim. Recently, Special Collection Service, a joint CIA-NSA program, had intercepted communications that the Brotherhood of Ali was planning to assassinate a high-value Western target, and Langley tasked Chris and Hannah to find out who was being targeted and who was going to do the hit. After examining available intel on the Brotherhood of Ali, Ozzie seemed like the easiest mark to lead them to the assassin and his target.

Near Hannah and Ozzie stood a bedraggled middle-aged businessman checking his watch and a perky young woman wearing a bright yellow head scarf, or *hijab*, texting on her smartphone. A policewoman donning her uniform cap over a black hijab hurried south on foot. Turkey's previous president had prohibited the hijab in government offices, but today's president, Recep Erdogan, allowed police officers and other civil servants to wear the head covering. Chris didn't have a problem with the hijab for government workers, but he did have a problem with President Erdogan repeatedly shutting down social media, jailing more journalists than any other country in the world, and declaring a state of emergency that continued for over a year, pushing Turkey's democracy closer and closer to a dictatorship—not good for a NATO country, or any country for that matter.

Chris smiled and waved to Hannah. She waved back. A week ago, when she had first met Ozzie at the stop, she asked an innocuous question: "When does the next tram arrive?" Each day, she engaged in light chit chat about the weather and so on, and each day, Chris picked her up in his sporty car. Sonny, the third member of Chris and Hannah's trio, remained hidden and shadowed Ozzie.

Ozzie started each morning here at Mescid-i Selam Station. Although he used various routes to arrive in Istanbul, he always ended at the Brotherhood of Ali's hangout, Mustafa Teahouse, where they gathered to drink, smoke, gossip, and conduct business.

But today was different—the tram was late. Unbeknownst to Ozzie, the tram was involved in a small "accident." Chris and Hannah, however, knew it was Sonny who'd caused the fender bender, and he wouldn't be tailing Ozzie today.

Hannah was to invite Ozzie to ride with her, and Chris was pleased to see them approach the Porsche together.

Chris rolled down the window.

"This is my new friend, Ozzie," Hannah said cheerfully. "His train is late—can we give him a ride?"

"Sure. Hi, I'm Chris Weston." He used his real first name, easy to remember, and an alias for a last name.

"Thank you," Ozzie said. His pronunciation sounded like *sank you*.

Hannah opened the back passenger door for him.

"This car looks great," Ozzie said.

Chris and Hannah smiled. *The fish was eyeing the bait.*

From earlier surveillance, Chris already knew Ozzie's destination, but he pretended not to. "Where you going?"

Ozzie hesitated. "Vatan." He often got off at Vatan and walked the two hundred and fifty meters to the Metro Ten Line. Now it would be easier for Ozzie to get dropped off directly at the Metro Ten, but he seemed to be careful not to give his exact destination.

Chris looked around for the policewoman or her fellow officers. No cops were in sight. He waited a moment for a car to turn off the road, and then he put the Porsche in gear and gassed it. The seats sucked Chris back, and the vehicle leaped forward. He glanced in the rearview mirror.

Ozzie smiled. "Ohh!" He grabbed the seat and said something in Turkish in a tone mixed with joy and fear. Behind the car, a trail of dust kicked up, infused with bright sunlight. Ozzie laughed like he was on a roller coaster ride.

Chris raced past restaurants, shops, and a gas station before braking for a turn. The deeper he drove into Istanbul, the newer the buildings were and the more congested the traffic became. He made another turn. "Hannah probably told you, but we're here in Istanbul doing some international trading."

"I work in computers," Ozzie said.

"Oh, what in computers?" Chris asked.

Ozzie shifted in his seat. "Computers."

"Ozzie is a private man," Hannah said.

"Of course," Chris said. "Well, maybe we can get together at my house sometime, or we can go out for dinner."

Ozzie didn't say anything.

Chris worried that he'd pushed too hard too soon, so he turned on the radio.

"What's a good radio station?" Hannah asked.

"FM 94.9," Ozzie said.

Hannah found the radio station. It played an eclectic mix of classical, rock, and hip-hop music, and soon they arrived at Vatan. Chris stopped in front of the tram station there and handed his business card to Ozzie. On it were the addresses and phone numbers of fronts for Chris's headquarters in Montreal and his European office in London—each with a real office where a secretary would greet visitors and answer phones and e-mail.

"Thank you," Ozzie said politely. He opened the door and stepped out.

"See you tomorrow," Hannah said.

Ozzie smiled. "Bye."

"Bye," Chris said. He pulled away from the curb and onto the street. "That didn't go so well," he mumbled.

"For a first meet, that went sweet," Hannah said. She was more experienced at the recruiting side of Agency work; Chris's forte was the paramilitary side.

Chris looked in the rearview mirror to see if anyone had followed them, or if the same vehicle showed up repeatedly. "We need to find out who the assassin and his target are."

"We will."

THE NEXT DAY, WHEN Hannah offered Ozzie a ride again, he took it. On the way to Vatan, listening to FM 94.9, Hannah said, "Ozzie, we're thinking about importing some computers, but we're no computer experts, and I was wondering if you might go out to dinner with us tonight and take a look at the specs."

Ozzie stared at her.

She smiled.

His face beamed brightly. "Sure."

"Shall we pick you up at Mescid-i Selam Station at six?" she asked.

"Six is good."

Chris dropped him off at Vatan.

———⊶◉⊷———

THAT EVENING, CHRIS and Hannah picked up Ozzie at the tram stop. This time, they drove him further into Istanbul. Across from the Italian Consulate stood a nineteenth-century building, originally a Franciscan monastery for nuns, which was now a hotel—the Tomtom Suites—warmly illuminated by the setting sun.

They strolled inside the four-story hotel and took the elevator to the top, where they located the Nicole restaurant. There Sonny already sat at a table. He'd arrived early to watch for anyone suspicious—especially a surveillance or ambush team. Like a chipmunk, his cheeks were stuffed with food. Red peppers, raspberries, and their juices lay on his plate like the scene of a messy murder. His cover as a casual diner was so convincing that Chris worried for a moment if he really was doing his job, but in situations like this, Sonny kept his head on a tactical swivel, and ultimately Chris had confidence in him. If the bullets started flying, Chris couldn't think of anyone else he'd rather have on his side.

Chris scanned the restaurant for possible threats, but nothing tingled his spider senses. A waitress greeted his party in Turkish, "*Hozgeldiniz*," which Chris recognized as "welcome," but he didn't understand the rest of what she said. Ozzie replied in Turkish. To Chris's horror, the waitress led them to a window seat—a good spot for a sniper to take them out. Chris asked, "Could we have a different table, please?"

"Yes," the waitress said in English.

"What wrong that table?" Ozzie asked.

"It's not clean," Hannah said.

Ozzie squinted at the clean table as if searching for the unclean spot. "Ah."

The waitress seated them at a table farther from the window. Hannah sat beside Ozzie and Chris across from them. "Would you like some wine?" Hannah asked Ozzie.

"Yes," he said.

"May I recommend a local white wine?" the waitress asked.

"Yes, for two please," Hannah said. A few drinks would help to loosen up Ozzie.

Ozzie looked at Chris and said, "Don't you want to drink?"

"I'm driving," Chris said. Even if he wasn't driving, he'd given up alcohol when he became a minister. Some pastors drank, but Chris wasn't one of them. Their waitress handed them bilingual menus in Turkish and English before leaving to give them some time to think about their orders.

Chris could see past the other patrons to the view outside. The sunlight dimmed, and the parks darkened, but soon lights flicked on, illuminating mosque domes and a minaret. Beyond them, ships on the Sea of Marmara glowed, passing to and fro between the Black Sea and the Aegean Sea—the same waters where the Argonaut heroes of Greek mythology sailed thousands of years ago.

Hannah's eyes sparkled like moonlight reflecting off the dark ocean, and Chris once again found himself within her depths. He was a part of the ocean and the ocean a part of him. The ebb and flow of the waves caressed him. He rose and fell with the swells—aware of the rhythm of his breathing. The sea kissed his soul, and he kept swimming. Eventually, his arms and legs weakened, and he began to sink. The sea gave life, and it took life, too. He returned to shore. On land, his body became heavy and off balance, and he had to sit down. He flapped the kinks out of his wrists and ankles. His strength and equilibrium returned, and he stood, staring at the sea one final time. No matter how seductively the ocean sparkled or how wonderful she made him feel, she could never be his. Sometimes he closed his eyes, and he continued to feel the push-pull of her waters, and he dreamed of diving deep. But he could never stay there. Although he was a former frog-man and comfortable with the water, his body required land, where he could run, climb rocks, and rappel down cliffs. It was where he belonged. He wanted to let go, but there was nothing that could compare to the ocean. He needed to let go. But once again he found himself at the water's edge.

The waitress brought their wine and took their orders before disappearing again.

Ozzie took a sip of his beverage. "Chris, may I ask personal question?"

"Sure," Chris said.

"Are you and Hannah—you know?"

Chris tried not to betray his astonishment at Ozzie's blunt question in Hannah's presence, but he quickly recalled from their briefings that the man simply was not experienced with women. He tried to sound convincing in his reply. "We're business partners. And friends. That's all."

Ozzie smiled. Then he glanced at Hannah.

She returned his smile.

The waitress brought out an amuse-bouche, followed by a *tarama* and watermelon salad. Ozzie's glass was empty, and Hannah's was half full. She ordered a refill for Ozzie.

"What do you like to do in your spare time, Ozzie?" she asked.

Ozzie spoke in a monotone with minimal eye contact: "A lot of indie concerts. And model building." Then he kept talking, as if reciting a list for an elementary school report. "I like play accordion and kazoo. I like jogging. I like work out and exercise. Play video games..."

"Oh," Hannah said politely. "Do you have a girlfriend?"

Chris and Hannah already knew the answer.

The waitress arrived and refilled Ozzie's glass with wine, and he took a sip. "No," he said.

Hannah could hold her liquor, and she played the spy vs. spy game of getting him to drink more. "What do you look for in a girl?" she asked.

He looked directly at her. "A girl who likes to party like me."

Chris was amused by Ozzie's attempt at bluster. He tried to hide his mood by taking a bite of his salad and covertly scanning nearby eyes and hands for threats. Eyes betray thoughts, which betray hands, which betray actions. A woman wearing a green blouse and no makeup had eyes with small pupils, like a snake about to strike, and she wielded her knife as if she might stab someone. The woman across from her chattered on as if oblivious to her dining partner's body language. Snake Eyes didn't seem to notice Chris or his table, and it didn't seem like she could do much damage with the table knife, so he continued to examine the room.

Sonny stuffed his serene face with lamb.

Chris grinned.

The other tables filled with customers. In the lobby, a fit man in a dark suit jacket, black polo shirt, and tan slacks sat patiently while others around him fidgeted and waited for a table. Chris pretended not to look at him but caught Black Polo looking his way—maybe it meant nothing; maybe it meant something.

The waitress brought out octopus seasoned with red peppers and raspberries, the same dish Sonny had massacred earlier. Hannah ordered red wine for Ozzie and herself.

Chris had eaten enough poorly prepared rubbery octopus to dislike it, but he needed to do something while he and Hannah waited for the effects of the wine to work on Ozzie. Once Ozzie got a good buzz going, Chris would make his pitch. In the meantime, he took a bite of his octopus. Surprisingly, it was tender and tasty.

After the red wine arrived and Ozzie was down to half a glass, Chris made his pitch. "Ozzie, a Kuwaiti businessman is selling used computers cheap, and Hannah and I have a buyer lined up in Brazil, where computers are quite expensive."

"It seems like a great deal," Hannah said, "but we were wondering if you might take a look at the specs and the price. See what you think."

Ozzie set his wine glass down. "Let me look."

Chris took out his iPhone and showed Ozzie a document with the numbers. They were slightly overpriced for used computers, and Chris hoped Ozzie would notice and say something about it.

"This sale is US dollars?" Ozzie asked.

"Yes," Chris replied.

"He overcharge you."

"Overcharging by how much?" Hannah asked.

Ozzie lifted his glass and took a drink. "If I buy these, I tell him take two hundred dollars off each."

"Wow," Chris said. "That's a significant difference, especially since we'll be buying and selling in bulk."

"Are you sure, Ozzie?" Hannah asked.

Ozzie drained his glass and set it on the table. "Yes. You might even ask cheaper."

"That's fantastic!" Chris said.

Hannah put her hand on Ozzie's shoulder. Chris didn't care for it, but her flirting with Ozzie was part of the bait. "Thank you, Ozzie," she said.

Tomorrow they would hook the fish.

Chapter Five

The next afternoon, Chris and Hannah picked up Ozzie. He still hadn't given them his home address or his work destination, but they already knew them. Chris pulled away from the curb and, after a few minutes of small talk, Hannah reached into the back seat and handed Ozzie an envelope.

He opened it. Inside was seven thousand Turkish liras, roughly equivalent to two thousand US dollars.

"I can't take this," Ozzie said.

"You made us a lot more than that by helping us negotiate this shipment of computers," Chris said. "In the future, I expect we'll sell even more used computers."

"This is simply a small way to show our gratitude," Hannah said.

Ozzie was unsophisticated, and now he had new friends, extra cash, the opportunity to make more money, and romantic possibilities. But even he seemed to sense the danger of the situation. He held the envelope in his hands and stared at it. He was on the edge.

Hannah smiled at him.

Ozzie looked at her hesitantly. Then he grinned broadly. He pocketed the money and gave her his cell phone number.

He took the bait! Chris wanted to jump out of his skin and celebrate, but he maintained a poker face and kept the Porsche between the ditches. Now it was time to use the little fish as bait to lure in the big fish—Brotherhood of Ali's assassin.

The following morning, Chris and Hannah didn't meet Ozzie at the tram stop. The business day after, they picked him up. This time, Hannah played quiet.

"Chris, what wrong with Hannah?" Ozzie said. "I asked her, but she not say. What happened?"

Chris let out a sigh as he steered round a curve. "Weeks ago, we shipped some cargo for a man who called himself the Kurd, but he refused to pay us, so we stopped doing business with him. Yesterday, he left a dead pigeon on Hannah's doorstep with a note that said if she didn't become his mistress, she'd become like the pigeon. It was signed, 'the Kurd.' She was so afraid, she wouldn't even leave her house yesterday." Chris and Hannah knew that Ozzie and the Brotherhood of Ali disliked the Kurds.

"Do you know this Kurd's name?" Ozzie asked.

"Huseyin Giyasettin," Chris said. "He recently emigrated from Iraq."

"Name not familiar," Ozzie said. "You talked to the police?"

Chris stopped at the light. "Should I?"

"No. I know someone who can take care of this."

"I don't know. The Kurd seemed pretty dangerous. Like mafia or something."

"Don't worry about the Kurdish mafia. Falcon can make this problem go away. Permanently." Ozzie put his hand on Hannah's shoulder.

Bingo! Chris thought. "His name is Falcon?"

"Not his real name."

"We don't want to do anything illegal," Chris said.

"You not do anything illegal," Ozzie said. "No worry."

"Maybe you can set up a meeting with Falcon at Nicole restaurant, and Hannah and I can be there, too—make like it's a coincidence. Maybe you could introduce us," Chris said.

"I don't know."

"Please," Hannah said weakly.

Ozzie gazed at her. "I'll see what I can do."

OZZIE SET UP A RENDEZVOUS for dinner a week later at Nicole. Sonny was the early bird again, already there with a meal when Chris and Hannah arrived precisely on time, 7:00 PM, but there was no sign of Ozzie or Falcon. This time, a different waitress greeted them.

"Could we have a table away from the window, please?" Chris asked.

"Yes, of course," the waitress said. After seating them, she brought menus and asked, "Would you like something to drink?"

"No, thank you," Hannah said.

Minutes ticked by, and Chris checked his phone for a text message from Ozzie, but there was none. The waitress returned and asked kindly, "Are you ready to order?"

Chris had no idea how late Ozzie would be, and he didn't want to finish eating before he arrived, so he stalled for time. There were only two courses on the menu, but he said, "Could we have some more time, please?"

"Certainly," she said before disappearing again.

More minutes went by.

"He's late," Hannah said.

"Yep."

The waitress returned. "Ready?" she asked.

"We're waiting for a friend," Chris said.

"Do you have any nonalcoholic drinks?" Hannah asked the waitress.

"We have ayran," she said.

"Two, please," Hannah said.

The waitress left.

Chris smiled.

"What?" Hannah asked.

"I just remembered the last time we were in Turkey," he said.

Hannah's eyes were bright and glossy. "When we were placed under arrest by our own consulate?"

"Yeah."

"I'm glad you can smile about it," she said.

"I can smile about it now, but I couldn't smile about it then."

"Insurgents torched the place. We were lucky to get out alive."

Chris remembered the brave men and women who died, and he stopped smiling. "Sonny saved us from that one." Chris glanced over at their buddy, who seemed blissfully lost in his dessert.

Ozzie walked through the door with a lean, hatchet-faced guy who had steely eyes and a hook nose that looked like it'd been broken more than once. *Falcon.* A waitress seated them.

Chris and Hannah pretended not to notice. Ozzie spotted them, too, but ignored them. Then Chris and Hannah's waitress brought their yogurt-flavored waters, and they ordered. After Ozzie and Falcon placed their orders, too, Ozzie said something to Falcon, and he looked at Chris and Hannah. Again, Chris and Hannah acted oblivious.

Sonny pretended to text on his phone, but he was taking photos of Ozzie's friend.

Then Ozzie and Falcon stood and came Chris and Hannah's way. Ozzie's walk was unsteady and unassertive. "Hannah, is that you?" Ozzie asked.

They looked up. "Ozzie!"

"This is my friend, Falcon," Ozzie said.

Falcon nodded courteously.

"I'm Chris, and this is Hannah."

"Hi," Hannah said.

Before anyone could say anything else, Falcon said something quietly in Turkish to Ozzie, who forced a smile at Chris and Hannah and said, "Bye." Then Ozzie and Falcon returned to their table.

Hannah sipped her ayran. "That was quick."

Chris took a drink, too. "I don't think Ozzie will pop the question."

"Even if he does, this guy doesn't seem the type to help out a stranger," Hannah said.

"We should put Falcon under surveillance."

Hannah nodded.

"I'll collect his DNA," Chris said.

The waitress brought their meal, and Chris and Hannah ate leisurely, waiting for Ozzie and Falcon to leave so Chris could collect a DNA sample from Falcon's dinnerware, and Sonny could follow him.

Falcon was a fast eater, and he finished his meal well before Ozzie did. Ozzie stopped eating and paid their check.

Chris had to collect the dinnerware after Ozzie and Falcon were gone but before a waitress cleared the table. His heart beat faster. Falcon sauntered through the exit with Ozzie in tow. Sonny followed them out, keeping his distance.

Chris stood and removed an empty envelope from his pocket. His heart hammered harder, and he strolled up to Ozzie and Falcon's empty seats. At the other tables, diners were focused on each other and their meals, and waiters and waitresses busily took orders and served customers. Chris swiped Falcon's spoon and fork, placed them in the paper envelope, pocketed it, and kept walking.

Chapter Six

In the dark hours of the Damascus morning, Max and his brother Tom rode in the back seat of a black Toyota Land Cruiser, popular with both NATO and terrorists for its reliability and sturdiness. Their driver was a long-bearded Free Syrian Army (FSA) man named Sami, who asked in fluent English, "You want to go directly to the position where our man got shot? It is one of the sniper's areas."

"Yes," Max said. "The closer we are to the sniper's location, the easier it'll be for us to hear and see him when he takes another shot."

Sami accelerated. "Can't you hear him and see him if you're farther away?"

"Not as well."

"We've been hunting for this sniper for a year," Sami said. "He has killed thirty warriors from my tribe. We call him the Ghost. He'll kill you, too."

I'm not your tribe, Max thought.

Sami wrapped his fingers around his long beard, as if trying to wrap his head around these counter-sniper tactics. "My men will set up in a two-story building. One of them is already there. You want to be *in* the building?"

Tom supported his brother: "*In* the building."

"What if the sniper shoots you?" Sami asked.

Max shrugged his shoulders. "There's always a downside." He and Tom had promised Sami's boss, a powerful local chieftain named Azrael, that they would rid him of a sniper if Azrael could give them information about a new assassination drug the Syrian government was working on. Azrael had provided good intel to CIA before, and Max hoped he'd provide good intel again. The Agency had received reports that such a drug would be used on a high-level target. Another team was working on the identities of the assassin and target, and Max and Tom were tasked with finding out about the drug.

Sami pulled off the road and skidded to a halt behind a drab two-story concrete building. "This is it," he said.

Max hopped out with his rucksack full of gear and hustled to the building. Tom's running footsteps sounded behind him. The Syrian sniper wouldn't begin work until sunrise, but Max didn't want to be surprised if the sniper clocked in early. Sami seemed to be of the same mind; he hustled, too.

A small young man opened the door for them. Max, Tom, and Sami hastened inside. The only light in the house came from moonlight through dingy curtains. They were in an unfurnished kitchen, and at the far end was a living room, also unfurnished, with some bedrolls rolled up against the wall. The plaster on the walls was chipped and cracked, and there were holes in the west wall that let in morning moonbeams. Off to the side was a bathroom.

Sami introduced the young man who'd let them in, "This is Jack. He's one of my men."

Max smiled at hearing the American name—or nickname. They shook hands, and Jack returned the smile.

Sami and Jack went to the far corner of the living room and discussed something. In the kitchen, Tom asked quietly, "What's wrong?"

"I want you up on the second floor with me sniping, but I don't trust these two guys to secure the first floor."

Tom bounced on his toes, ready to get to it. "I'll help them secure the first floor."

"If any of them even look sideways at you or seem the least bit squirrelly, you let me know, and we're out of here pronto. And if I see anything squirrelly, no discussions—we grab our kit and go." Kit was what they called their gear.

"You don't trust them."

"Not with my life," Max said. "And certainly not with yours."

Tom nodded.

Armed with a highly customized AK, Max hauled his sniper rifle and kit upstairs. He would use the AK for close-in fighting if needed and the sniper rifle for longer distances. His gear included a small SE (Site Exploitation) kit—a Q-tip and collection bag with which to obtain the target's DNA. He could use his phone to take a photograph of the body.

He checked out his digs. The deck leaned to one side and sagged in spots. He spotted one empty room—then another. Similar to downstairs, there were holes in the west wall here, too—big like a .50-caliber machine gun with ADD had been making Swiss cheese before becoming distracted and moving on to something else.

Max lay down and looked through one hole that caught his eye. It was wide enough for him to see through with his scope and shoot straight through. The more he backed away from the orifice, the more wall he could see and the less outdoors he could observe. He'd have to keep his muzzle close to the hole to maximize his view of the city. However, the wall was thick—even with his muzzle fixed in one spot, he couldn't pivot the neck of the barrel left, right, up, or down without plaster blocking his movement. He decided to leave the edges of the outdoors side of the hole as is but widen his side of the hole. He took out his mini-tool knife and unfolded the blade. Then he picked, hacked, and carved away at the plaster until his side of the hole became bigger.

Next, he laid down his AK and unpacked a Russian SVD sniper rifle. Without the bipod attached, the weapon would be too low to shoot through the hole, and with a bipod attached, it'd sit too high. He could knock out another hole in the wall at the correct height, and maybe the enemy sniper wouldn't recognize a new hole—but maybe he would.

Footsteps sounded from the stairway and Sami came in the room. "Is everything okay?"

Max remembered the bedrolls downstairs. "Where there's a will, there's a way," he said in English.

Sami had fluent English, but maybe he hadn't learned all the American idioms. He stared at Max blankly.

Max translated into Arabic: *Hayth hunak 'iiradat hunak wasila.*

Sami's eyes brightened, and he nodded.

Max went downstairs, grabbed two bedrolls, and dragged them upstairs. He laid one down on the deck for him to lie on and folded the other until it supported his aim, sans bipod.

He peered through his scope. The sky had turned from the black of the void to dark gray, and shadows materialized into buildings and cars.

Vehicles rumbled outside and stopped near their building. Max's heart seemed to skip a beat, and his breathing paused.

"My guys are here," Sami said.

Max's heart rate and breathing became normal again.

Sami hurried downstairs. The door unlocked and opened. Feet trampled inside, and men's voices chattered loudly as if they were on a vacation. Max was pissed at their lack of professionalism. Then came the bittersweet smell of tobacco. If the sniper couldn't hear these morons, he could see the glow of their cigarettes. But getting all worked up wouldn't help Max do his job, so he searched for a silver lining. On the positive side, if the sniper was out there, he'd certainly take a shot at one of these yahoos. Then Max would take his shot. *Sniper bait.*

Some of the men stayed downstairs, smoking and chatting, and a few others climbed the stairs. "We're going to set up an observation post on the roof," Sami said.

"Knock yourselves out," Max said.

Sami's buddies stomped around on the roof like a small herd of cattle. Then they quieted down a bit but not completely—if one guy wasn't moving up there, another was talking. *These guys will never win the war against Assad.*

Two of a sniper's greatest considerations are wind and distance. There was no wind, so Max didn't have to worry about that. He did have to worry about distance. From his pocket, he pulled out his iPhone, which contained his sniper data. He reached into his rucksack and took out a pair of Leica Vector binoculars. Training them on the distant terrain, he noted a road about a hundred meters away. A cargo truck stopped, and Max used the range finder of his binoculars to bounce a laser off the broad side of it. He read the digital readout in his binoculars—*ninety-five meters*. Then he entered the data into his iPhone. Farther out, he lazed a clump of houses—*two hundred and eight meters*. A little farther was a neighborhood mosque with a good view of its surroundings—an obvious choice for a sniper, though probably too obvious—*two hundred and sixty-eight meters*. At five hundred and thirty-six meters was a hospital. Fifty meters beyond that was a soccer stadium, which would make an excellent sniper platform—especially with a labyrinth of entrances and exits for the sniper's escape. Max couldn't imagine a Syrian sniper engaging from farther away than the soccer stadium. If Max were the sniper, he'd use the stadium.

While he waited for the sniper to make his next move, he simulated acquiring a target in one of the arches of the soccer stadium. He held high to compensate for the distance. Instead of waiting for the natural stillness between exhaling and inhaling, Max paused his breathing and squeezed—steady and straight. *Click.* Then he switched it up—imagining a car stop beside the road and the flash of a sniper's scope. Max held low to compensate for the closeness. *Click.* Satisfied with his quick dry-fire exercise, he chambered a round and waited.

The sun broke the horizon, and calls to prayer rang from loudspeakers at mosques throughout Damascus, creating an abstract song. *Smack!* A bullet struck something, or someone, on the roof. Though startled, Max's training and experience kicked in, and he began counting off seconds between the impact upstairs and the report of the rifle. Before he finished counting off one second, the rifle went *bang*. Because each second between the shot hitting near him and the report of the rifle equaled three hundred meters, this sniper was a bit less than three hundred meters away. *Close.* It came from the direction of the mosque.

Max pivoted his rifle in the direction of the mosque and methodically examined each opening and nook. *No sniper.* He checked the surrounding area. A man wearing black Adidas sweatpants and a black T-shirt and holding a rifle down to his side ran from the building. Max tried to get his crosshairs on him, but he disappeared behind another structure—like an apparition. *Damn!*

Sami and the herd of men upstairs ran and stumbled downstairs, hollering all the way down to the first floor, except for Sami, who stopped in Max's room.

"Is anyone shot?" Max asked.

"No," Sami said. "Did you get the sniper?"

Max was embarrassed. "No."

The sun heated the city, and the rest of the day Max took turns watching with Tom. When sunset neared, they became especially vigilant, but there were no more signs of the sniper.

Before dawn the next morning, Sami and his buddies returned to the roof. This time they crept up stealthily.

Max's father, a Marine Force Recon sniper, had taught Max and Tom the finer points of camouflage, stalking, and shooting at a young age. Later, Max became a SEAL, and after he deployed to Ramadi, Iraq with SEAL Team Three, he returned to the States and graduated from SEAL sniper school. When he earned a spot in Development Group, one of a growing list of aliases for SEAL Team Six, the Team's sniper slots were full, so he served as an assaulter. After a combat tour with DEVGRU, he left the Navy and joined CIA Special Activities Division/Special Operations Group, the tip of the tip of the spear. When the US wanted to send their best, they sent SEAL Team Six or Delta Force, but when they wanted to send their best and deny any knowledge of it, they sent Special Operations Group. In spite of all of Max's training and combat experience, he'd never killed an enemy sniper.

He scanned the mosque's gray silhouette and its surrounding area, checking to see if the sniper would press his luck enough to show up there again. After several minutes of patient scanning, he noticed movement in the minaret. Max aimed. The view in his scope showed a man wearing a black T-shirt. *Is this the sniper? Or some harmless cleric?* Then Max spotted a long rifle mounted with a scope aimed in his direction.

Adrenaline dumped into Max's system, threatening to throw him off balance. In the faint light of dawn and from this distance, the sniper's chest presented the biggest target. Max took a long, deep breath to return to Happy Valley and aimed. *He must feel like king of the hill in his sniper hide.* It was time to overthrow the king, and the king had no idea it was coming. Max aligned his crosshairs on the man's chest. The sniper's muzzle flashed. Max squeezed the trigger. Max's brain couldn't process the sound of the sniper's shot or his own, but he recognized the satisfying recoil of his rifle butt into his shoulder. The sniper sank out of view. This time, the sniper didn't run out of the building. *Au revoir.*

The upstairs herd ran downstairs again, except for Sami, who stopped to see Max again.

"Anyone shot?" Max asked.

"No. Did you get him?" Sami asked.

Max nodded.

"Praise to Allah!" Sami cheered. "Praise to Allah." Then he ran downstairs and spread the news.

"Allah's got nothing to do with it," Max grumbled, but Sami was gone. Max packed his sniper rifle away and picked up his AK assault rifle.

On loudspeakers throughout the city, the cacophony of calls to morning prayer went out.

Max descended the steps to the first floor. Sami and his men jumped up and down and shouted praise to Allah. Tom high-fived Max, who smiled so hard that his face felt as if it might crack.

Tom leaned forward. "We should go ID the sniper."

"Yeah, before his buddies get to him and remove the body," Max said. He turned to Sami. "We're going to gather some intel from the sniper's body. You and your guys stand by here in case we need backup. If there are no problems, we'll return. We'll say 'Sami and Jack,' and you'll know it's us before you open the door."

Sami was still bouncing up and down and smiling. "Yes, yes, Sami and Jack. Praise Allah."

Religious nuts, Max thought, but he knew he might still need these religious nuts, so he didn't utter it.

Sami unlocked the back door, and Max and Tom exited. The door locked behind them with a loud click. Tom at his side, Max hoofed it around a graveyard of gutted buildings. He paused to examine a massive pile of busted-up concrete and dirt with weeds growing out of it—it was if someone with a tractor loader had picked up the remains of the destroyed buildings and dumped them in the courtyard. Max jogged around the mound of concrete in the courtyard and into an abandoned structure with half of its walls missing and no roof. He stepped lightly past an apartment building where a few of the lights were on and voices of an arguing couple emanated from within. He continued to shadow the couple's building as it extended under an overpass. At a busy road, he waited for a break in the headlights, and then he crossed, Tom close behind.

Max crept to the back of the mosque and found a brown door adorned with square shapes stacked on top of each other, each square filled with more intricate designs. He turned the doorknob—it was locked. He could go soft and pick the lock. On the other hand, there were no hinges on the outside, meaning that the door swung inward. He'd already made noise exchanging shots with the sniper, and time was wasting, so he went hard and kicked close to the doorknob. *Crack.* The door burst open. *Bang.* The door hit the wall.

The rear interior of the mosque was dark, but the front was well lit. Max located the stairs to the minaret and sneaked up them. At the top of the stairs, a cleric stood over a body lying in a dark puddle on the deck. Max and Tom aimed at him.

The cleric turned to them and shouted, "What are you doing in Allah's place of worship?!"

"*Masaa' al-khayr,*" Max said. Good evening.

"You can't bring weapons in here!" the cleric shouted.

Max pointed at the dead sniper. "Should've told him that."

Tom motioned for the cleric to step away from the body. Reluctantly, he did.

Then Max ordered him in Arabic: "Turn around and sit with your hands behind your back so I can see them." The cleric huffed and puffed but complied. In Max's line of work, there were talkers and fighters, and this cleric was a talker.

Just to be safe, Tom aimed his AK at the cleric while Max searched him for weapons—none. He confiscated the cleric's cell phone. "Wait, you can't take that," the man protested.

Max ignored him.

While Tom continued to train his weapon on the cleric, Max turned the body over and was startled by what he saw. "What the hell, he's white!" Max took out his own cell phone to snap a close-up photo, but he was so jacked up at having killed a sniper and so surprised that the sniper was white that he had a hard time keeping his hand steady. He took the picture.

"Is he European?" Tom asked.

"Don't know." Max turned the sniper's head and took his profile. Next, he snapped a full body photo. Then Max encrypted the photo and sent it to his CIA boss, Willy, a Cajun good-ole-boy and old family friend who treated Max and Tom as if they were the sons he never had.

Finally, Max took a Q-tip and swabbed some of the blood from the sniper's chest for a DNA sample, which he sealed in a collection bag and pocketed.

ID done, Max picked up the sniper's rifle, a Russian SVD similar to his own, and ejected the round from the chamber. In the world of snipers, now Max held the round that was meant for him; now he was immortal. He put it in his pocket. He'd become a combat HOG—Hunter of Gunmen. His father had been a HOG, too, but he was dead. Becoming immortal was only a superstition.

"Dad would be proud," Tom said quietly in French, disguising their American nationality.

"The world isn't the same without him in it," Max said.

"I miss him, too."

Max took the sniper's rifle so no one else could use it, and he told the cleric, "Don't go downstairs until the next call to prayer, or we'll shoot you."

With that, Max and Tom went downstairs and quietly left the mosque.

But a question gnawed at Max: *Who is this sniper?*

Chapter Seven

Max and Tom rumbled through the streets of Jobar in the back seat of a Toyota Land Cruiser with Sami at the wheel. The rising sun lit parts of the streets in gray, which alternated with the blackness created in the shadows of bombed-out buildings. Max felt as if they were traveling across an abstract chessboard.

Sami said, "This time, Azrael wants to meet you at his place. It is a wonderful honor for you.

Their Toyota truck continued with the power of a rook, capable of taking out obstacles that stood in their way. In this game of chess, there were multiple kings belonging to various tribes, and it was common for battles to break out among pieces of the same color.

Sami drove along a twisted road to a fortress wall, where they parked and got out. He led them to an iron gate, where a guard waved them through. In the middle of a spacious courtyard gurgled a star-shaped fountain, and beyond it stood a kingly marble palace with long, narrow vertical windows. Another guard greeted them in Arabic and ushered them inside. Seven meters above, the ceiling of the entrance-way was decorated with a massive honeycomb, called *muqarna*.

Music played, and Max was gobsmacked. "Is that reggae?" he whispered.

"Sounds like Bob Marley," Tom said.

Max preferred the classic rock of groups like AC/DC over reggae, but he recognized this song, "I Shot the Sheriff," and he liked it.

Sami escorted the brothers along a red carpet, under a golden chandelier, and through a wide hall lined on both sides with mirrors, repeating their images to infinity. The red carpet spilled into a living room where black velvet tapestries hung from the ceiling. The only light came from moonbeams passing through scarlet-tinted windows, shining a bloody hue inside the room. The pendulum of a massive ebony clock swung heavily as it ticked off each second.

On a black velvet sofa sat Azrael, a man in his thirties, who looked like Omar Sharif in *Lawrence of Arabia,* but he wore a dark suit and a Saddam Hussein moustache. Leisurely, he puffed a Cuban cigar before setting it down on a crystal ashtray on the end table next to him. Beside the ashtray was a glass of dark golden amber liquid in a whiskey glass and a bottle of Jim Beam Black. Azrael flashed a wicked smile before he took a sip.

He might be evil, but he's got good taste in whiskey, Max thought.

On the panoramic TV screen in front of him played a grainy black-and-white video of Saddam Hussein's 1979 Ba'ath Party Purge. Hussein called about four hundred of his leaders into an auditorium and made one of them, whom he'd tortured, announce the name of a traitor, and the "traitor" was taken from the room. One by one, more traitors were announced and arrested, and they departed with confusion and fear on their faces. Max didn't have to see the rest of the video to know how it ended. Sixty-eight in all would be arrested. Hussein would congratulate the leaders remaining in the auditorium. Soon twenty-two of those arrested were found guilty of treason. The forty-six who were spared were ordered to execute the twenty-two. Shortly after, hundreds more would be executed, and Hussein took control of Iraq. There was no sound on the video, only Bob Marley's reggae and the ticking of the pendulum. Max's stomach knotted itself.

In Arabic, Azrael's name meant "angel of death." He motioned for Sami to fetch two whiskey glasses.

"No, thank you," Tom said.

Max wanted a drink of the Jim Beam Black, but he supported his brother this time. "We're on duty."

Sami brought the glasses and set them on the table beside Azrael, who poured whiskey into them from his bottle. Then he held out the glasses to his guests.

Max took one and savored its oak fragrance, but Tom hesitated.

Azrael spoke cultured English without a noticeable accent: "It is polite to refuse once, but it is rude to refuse twice."

Max gave his brother a hard look: *Dude, take the drink.*

Reluctantly, Tom accepted the drink.

"Sami told me that you two got the sniper," Azrael said. He held his drink up in a toast. "Well done."

"*Fi sihtik,*" Max said in Arabic.

"*Fi sihtik,*" Tom repeated.

"Cheers," Azrael said.

The three of them took a drink. The Kentucky bourbon went down Max's throat creamy smooth, with a taste of caramel.

"When we spoke on the phone, you said the sniper was Syrian, but he didn't look Syrian," Max said in Arabic.

Azrael switched to his native Arab tongue. "I said he worked for the Syrian government, but I did not say he was Syrian."

Max and Tom took another drink. "You should've told us he wasn't Syrian," Max said.

Azrael drank, too. "Okay, I will tell you now. He was Russian."

Max's muscles stiffened.

Tom had a dazed look in his eyes, as if he'd been struck with a stun grenade.

Azrael seemed to notice their surprise. "If I had told you earlier, you might not have killed him."

"You lied," Max said. "Are you trying to start a war between us and the Russians?"

Azrael remained cool and calm. "He was killing my men. I did what I had to. Survival in Damascus is a complex business. I do not know why I expect Americans to understand that."

Two surly men entered the room, and one asked, "Is everything okay, Boss?"

Azrael waved them off, and they left the room.

Tom looked around at the place. "You seem to be doing better than surviving."

The furnishings appeared expensive and Max agreed with his brother. "Business is booming."

Sami stood still in the corner of the room like a potted plant, and Max and Tom handed their empty glasses to him.

Azrael set down his glass, picked up his cigar, and had a smoke. "The name of the new assassination poison you seek is BK-16. A man known as the Surgeon experiments with it on captured enemies of Assad's dictatorship. Some of my men were captured and experimented on—none of them survived. It is rumored that the Surgeon conducts his experiments at a location known as Hospital 175."

Max waited for Azrael to say more.

"That is all," Azrael said.

"We just killed a Russian sniper for you, and that's the best intel you can give us?"

"I am working on it," Azrael said. "As soon as I find out more, I will let you know."

Max clenched his fist in disgust, and he wanted to coldcock Azrael. He felt like he'd just been screwed by the devil.

Chapter Eight

After killing the Turkish gendarme, Minotaur ducked into the Russian consulate in Istanbul, where he lay low for a few days. The Rezidentura, the FSB officer who headed operations in Turkey, outranked Minotaur. Even so, Minotaur reported directly to Moscow, and the Rezidentura's responsibility was to support Minotaur, not supervise him. The Rezidentura told Minotaur that a young Spetsnaz sniper assigned to harass anti-Assad forces in Damascus had been killed, and Moscow's orders were for Minotaur to sail to Syria, find whoever killed the Spetsnaz sniper, and terminate him.

Minotaur sailed through the night on a medium-sized supply ship and arrived at the Russian naval base in Tartus, Syria. On the pier sat a black Toyota Land Cruiser with exhaust clouding up behind it. Minotaur disembarked the ship, sauntered to the truck, and tossed his kit in the back. Then he sat in the passenger seat. "Long time no see."

The man in the driver's seat was Bear. His real name was Orel Oglyevich. In 2011, he and Minotaur had tracked down and killed some of the Islamic terrorists responsible for the bombing at Russia's Domodedovo International Airport. Then and now, Bear's steel paunch pushed out his black T-shirt and hung over the waist of his blue jeans. He looked more like a good old American country boy than a Spetsnaz operator, but Bear was one of the deadliest commandos Minotaur knew. A permanent scowl on his face, Bear didn't smile for anyone. He carried a Serbu Super Shorty Remington 870 shotgun concealed in a shoulder holster that could swing out for immediate use.

Minotaur discreetly studied Bear. "I've been meaning to ask you—that shotgun only carries three rounds—what do you do if you run into more than three enemies?"

Bear put the vehicle in drive. "I've got six extra rounds mounted on a sidesaddle. If I need more than that, there'll be plenty of weapons lying on the ground to choose from."

Minotaur smiled. "Any new intel on the countersniper who shot our sniper?"

"I found someone who might know something." Bear's window was rolled down and he spit tobacco juice as if he'd chewed someone up and spit out their blood. "I'll take you to him."

In a fair fight, Bear would likely kill Minotaur—but Minotaur never fought fair. He was happy that Bear was on his side.

It was a short drive across base, where Bear parked at one of the warehouses. Bear got out of the SUV, and Minotaur followed him to a warehouse door. Bear unlocked it. Then the pair walked inside.

The interior was dark and smelled like tar, and Bear hit a switch. A dim light burned. Then Bear locked the door behind them.

Next to a pile of rope, a gagged man hung upside down, locked into a pair of gravity boots. He had a thick Stalin moustache. Bear introduced him: "This is Azrael, King of Damascus." Then Bear removed the ball gag.

"You capture him all by yourself?" Minotaur asked.

Bear spit tobacco juice on the deck. "Yep."

Minotaur smiled. "Gravity boots—so eighties—I like it. How long has he been upside down?"

Bear showed three fingers.

"Three hours." Minotaur leaned toward the man and looked down on him. "Every king should know what goes on in his kingdom, don't you agree?"

Azrael said nothing, but his breathing was labored, and there was fear in his eyes.

"I understand," Minotaur said. "Your vision is blurred, and your heart has to work harder because you're upside down. All that blood is starting to accumulate in your brain, and your heart can't pump it all out—that's why I'm sure that your head hurts. And your brain might be hemorrhaging. Your blood pressure will continue to rise—soon you'll have a stroke. But I think the greatest danger is the pressure on your lungs, causing asphyxiation. That's why you're struggling to breathe."

Azrael wheezed. "I know who killed your sniper."

"Who?"

"Let me down and I'll tell you," Azrael said.

"You tell me, and I'll let you down."

"Two Caucasian men in their late twenties, about six feet tall and fit," Azrael said. "They spoke Arabic."

"Anything else?"

"They wanted information about the BK-16 virus."

"And?"

Azrael caught his breath. "That is all."

"For a king, you don't know very much about your kingdom," Minotaur said. He nodded at Bear, signaling that they were finished.

With one hand, Bear pulled out a knife and flicked open a long, thick blade.

Azrael jerked with surprise, and the intonation rose in his words: "You do not have to worry about those two anymore. I poisoned them with BK-16. Gave them drinks from a bottle of whiskey laced with it."

"Now why would you do a thing like that?"

"I wanted to show your people that I'm on Russia's side."

Minotaur ground his teeth. "I think you're lying. I think you had those two kill our sniper. Then you poisoned the two men to remove the evidence of your actions. Avoid having to repay them."

Azrael continued to plead his case. "I had nothing to do with your sniper's death—I swear."

"I don't care whether you did or you didn't. And you shouldn't have BK-16—it's not yours to have."

"This isn't necessary."

Minotaur's pulse sped up, and his heart pounded hard. "That's what so many of them say."

"What?" Azrael asked.

"This isn't necessary."

You could release me, and you'll never see me again."

"I could. In Istanbul, I considered it—releasing a man."

"What happened?"

"I was in a bar where a Turk stared at me the whole time I was there. It was an ugly stare, as if he wanted to beat me up. His buddies were laughing—they thought it was funny. I couldn't stay in the bar all night, so I got up to leave. When I walked past them, he continued to stare, and his friends kept laughing. You know what I did next?"

"I think I know."

"I kept walking. It was freeing to know that I could ignore him. If I wanted to. When I reached the door, he was still staring and his friends laughing. I didn't want them to get the wrong impression—that I was leaving because of them. I wanted them to know I had choices—choices that they didn't have. So I motioned for the staring man to come outside and join me. I wanted to show him and his friends. I went outside. There I waited, breathing in the city air. The staring man and his friends came out, and I punched him once in the temple, and he died. His friends went to him and tried to revive him. They thought he still had choices, but he didn't. They couldn't understand he was dead. They said some of the same things to him in Turkish. And some different things. They tried to wake him up—slapped his face. But it was no use. I was bored and didn't wait to see their final realization of the situation."

Azrael's red face seemed to brighten. "You have choices."

"Yes."

Azrael wiggled and struggled for each breath. "I can get anything you want in Damascus."

"So can I." Minotaur casually studied his prey and experienced a rush of rhapsody. He enjoyed watching Azrael squirm—enjoyed hearing his last words. He'd seen it all, and he was sure Azrael had seen it all, too. "You think we're alike, but we're not. You're greedy; I'm simple. But you can't understand that."

"I can give you part of Damascus," Azrael said.

"What would I do with part of a city? You should accept your fate. It would be far nobler. I'm giving you that choice."

"I can pay you money, twenty-one thousand dollars," Azrael huffed and puffed. "From my safe at home."

Minotaur looked down on him. Syrian currency had dropped so low in value that people had to carry thick stacks of cash in order to go shopping. "Syrian money?"

Azrael continued to breathe heavily. "American."

"American," Minotaur said as if it put a sour taste in his mouth.

Azrael gasped for air. "What currency do you want?"

"This." Minotaur turned and nodded at Bear once more, who charged forward and slashed Azrael's throat.

Azrael's body threw itself into spasms, and he screamed. "Aarglh!" Crimson liquid spurted from his neck—more than usual because he was upside down. He flapped and twisted like a fish on a hook, choking on his blood, and his excited state made him bleed out faster.

The blood on Minotaur's hand felt soothingly warm. "Let's find one of Azrael's underlings and confirm his story about the two men who killed our sniper."

Chapter Nine

Tom had a vague feeling that he was dead. An indeterminate hum droned through the blackness of a dream, and he experienced a rumbling in his bones and the beat of his heart. *Maybe I'm still alive.*

He lay on something hard, and dust choked him. He feared what he might see if he opened his eyes, but more than that, he feared what he might not see. He clawed his way toward consciousness.

A faint light appeared in the corner of the darkness and spread until black lines took shape and became the legs of three Arab men. They appeared to be in their late twenties, like Tom. They were seated in the back of a truck, exposed to the elements. Tom attempted to move his hands swiftly, but there was a fog between his brain's command and his hands' response. Making matters worse, his hands were cuffed behind him. He struggled to his knees before he rose unsteadily and sat beside one of the men on a bench. Their hands were behind their backs, too. Tom's vision was still fuzzy, but he could see tilted palm trees and buildings as gravity pulled him down. *Where am I?*

The sunlight gradually brightened. He remembered that the Agency had sent his brother Max and him to Syria to investigate reports of a new drug to be used as part of some high-level assassination plot. And he remembered Max killing a Russian sniper for Azrael to get more information. They met with Azrael in the morning, and in the evening, they ate dinner at a restaurant in Jobar, a municipality of Damascus—the last thing that Tom remembered. Somehow he must've passed out.

Where's Max?

Tom's vision became clearer, and he spotted a truck in front of them and a truck behind—they were in a three-vehicle convoy. Inside Tom's truck, one man said to a bearded man, "I wouldn't be here if it weren't for you two. They were looking for you, but they captured me, too. Even though I'm innocent."

"You deserted Daesh," Long Beard said, using the pejorative word for the terrorist group.

The guy shook his head. "I didn't desert. I served my time, and then I left. I did my duty."

Long Beard grinned as if he were looking down on a child. "You came here for some adventure—isn't this adventurous?"

"They wouldn't have noticed me missing if they hadn't been looking for you two. It's you they want, not me."

"Daesh wants all of us. And they got us."

Tom's worst fear was realized—he was a prisoner of Daesh, aka ISIS. His breathing became rapid and shallow, and dust mixed in the air, complicating his breathing even more. Sweat drenched his body. The atmosphere felt oppressive. He had to get a grip before his life slipped away.

Deserter struggled with his cuffs, as if to free himself. "This isn't real, this isn't real."

The third prisoner had a thin neck. He leaned toward Long Beard and looked at Tom sideways. "Who is he?"

Long Beard eyed Tom and asked in Arabic, "Are you Russian? Or American?"

Tom weighed how to answer the question or if he should answer at all.

Deserter struggled harder and twitched as if he was losing his marbles. "Allah, help me."

"Shut up back there!" the driver barked.

Beside the road, a Syrian girl in a cinnamon-colored dress pointed at the convoy, but her mother pulled her into the house.

The trucks slowed.

"Why're we slowing down?" Deserter asked.

Long Beard chuckled at him as if he were an idiot. "End of the road."

The trucks stopped, and a guard armed with an AK-47 opened the back. "Get out!"

"Come on," Long Beard said. "Let's show them some pride."

Deserter balked and wouldn't leave the vehicle.

"Die with dignity, Deserter," Thin Neck growled.

Panic filled the deserter's voice. "Tell them I'm not FSA," referring to Free Syrian Army, the enemies of Daesh and President Assad's dictatorship. Tom assumed that Long Beard and Thin Neck *were* FSA.

"He's not FSA," Long Beard said.

Deserter appealed to the guard. "See?"

The guard snatched him off the truck. "Off the truck, deserter!"

Deserter fell and stayed on the ground. "No, I'm not a deserter," he pleaded. "You're wrong."

"Shut up!" the guard barked.

"No, no, no!" Deserter leaped to his feet and ran past the guard.

"Stop!" The guard brought up his AK-47 and pointed it at the fleeing man.

"You can't execute me for desertion because I'm not deserting!" He kept running.

The guard's muzzle flashed. *Pa-pa-pa-pa-pow!* Deserter arched his back before he crashed into the dust. The guard closed in on him, and Deserter wiggled as if to get away. The guard fired on full auto again. Gore sprayed and Deserter became still.

The guard turned and sneered at Tom and the others and asked, "Who wants to escape next?"

The specter of death hovered over Tom, and his chest tightened. He was afraid—which meant he was still alive. Even so, how he handled fear could extend his life or terminate it. He remembered his father teaching him to breathe "four-and-four-for-four" to help him through stressful situations. So Tom breathed in for four seconds and exhaled for four more seconds. As he continued his four-and-four-for-four, he made a snap inventory of his person: his belt was gone, and he couldn't feel the pressure of his concealed pistol against his abdomen. Similarly, his pockets seemed empty, and his knife was missing, too. Daesh had taken everything. Or so it seemed.

He touched the back hem of the waist of his trousers—his razor blade in a tiny sheath and lock pick were still hidden inside, and he knew he could use the pick to unlock his handcuffs. He pushed the fingers of both hands inside his waistband and felt for a piece of fabric to pull. He rapidly found it. With the fingers of one hand he pulled—coughing to conceal the sound of the Velcro opening—while he held the fingers of his other hand below the lock pick to catch it. As he opened the hem further the razor and metal shim fell into his fingers. The metal of the pick was warm like his handcuffs.

The guard who shot the deserter seemed to have a permanent sneer, and he sauntered to the prisoners' truck as if he was the leader. "Out!" he barked.

Long Beard hopped out of the vehicle, and Thin Neck followed. Tom's white skin and six-foot height made him stand out enough as it was, and he didn't want to draw more attention to himself by appearing disobedient, so he got out of the truck briskly. He didn't want to lose his precious pick, and he squeezed his fingers tightly. When his feet hit the ground, his body jolted, and he dropped something. *The razor.* He hoped he wouldn't be needing it. Moreover, he hoped his captors didn't notice it in the dirt.

"Follow me," the leader said.

Tom had witnessed numerous videos of the horrors of ISIS executions—images and audio unavailable to the public, too grisly to speak of, except in a whisper. He forgot about four-and-four-for-four. The manner and moment of his death consumed him.

Tom and his fellow prisoners followed the leader to an open area surrounded by buildings, where a black-clad man gripping an ax stood next to a chopping block, blood-stained wicker basket, and an ISIS flag. The blade of the ax was longer than any Tom had seen before—custom forged, it was horrifically beautiful. Opposite the executioner stood a man with a digital camera mounted on a tripod. Black-clad men armed with AKs stood around, but it wasn't clear whether they were additional muscle, spectators, or what their purpose was. A fire smoldered in a barrel, its smoke stinking like burned human excrement.

The terrorist leader put his hands on his hips and stared at the Arab prisoners. "You call yourselves the Free Syrian Army, but we will free Damascus, not you."

Tom covertly slipped his pick into a cuff lock and turned it. His cuff unlocked.

"Did you hear something?" the executioner asked, his voice booming and menacing.

The executioner's words struck Tom like a lightning bolt of fear.

"I didn't hear anything," the leader said. "To the chopping block."

The sound of machines began to rumble, grind, whoosh and buzz. There must've been a construction crew clearing debris nearby. Tom wished the construction work had started earlier to mask the sound of him unlocking his cuffs.

When it was his turn to die, Tom planned to bow as if he was about to kneel to the block before sprinting between the two nearest buildings. Outnumbered and unarmed, he didn't expect to get far before Daesh gunned him down, but at least he'd go out resisting. His mother had died when he was young, his girlfriend died several months ago, and his father was killed soon after. Now he looked forward to reuniting with all three of them. His heartbeat slowed, his breathing calmed, and his mind cleared. Thinking of meeting them on the other side made him tranquil. *See you soon.*

The leader stood in front of the camera and ranted, "Allah's enemies are the apostates, Free Syrian Army, Shiites, atheists, Christians, and Jews. Today we have captured three of them, and we capture more each day. Allah's enemies cannot stop Damascus from becoming another base under *our* Caliphate...

Thin Neck sighed loudly. "Are you going to shut up and do this or kill me with your boring speech?"

The leader's sneer faded, and he became flustered. "Cut, cut," he commanded the cameraman before turning to Thin Neck and shouting, "You first!"

Thin Neck reverently approached the chopping block and stood.

"Roll camera," the leader said.

Thin Neck looked up at the leader and said, "Allah loves me. Can you say the same for yourself, infidel?"

The leader screamed at the cameraman, "Cut, cut!" Then he screamed at Thin Neck, "No more talking!"

"Yes, please," Thin Neck said. "No more talking."

"You don't hear it?" the executioner said.

"I don't hear anything except you and this yapping dog," the leader barked. "And the racket from that construction crew." He took a moment to cool down. "Roll camera."

Thin Neck kneeled and bowed his head to the chopping block.

The executioner swung his ax through the air and chopped off Thin Neck's head. Tom's stomach roiled as he watched it topple into the bloody basket. The leader kicked the headless body over to the side, and two of his men dragged it away.

"He died as he lived," Long Beard said in a mournful baritone. "Fearless."

Tom silently recited the Lord's Prayer: *Our Father who art in heaven, Hallowed be thy name. Thy kingdom come. Thy will be done, in earth, as it is in heaven...*

The leader pointed at Tom. "Next!"

Tom walked to the chopping block.

...and lead us not into temptation, but deliver us from evil...

Out of the corner of his eye, Tom eyed the space between the two buildings where he planned to run. He bowed as if about to kneel. He unlocked his other cuff. *Clang.* His handcuffs fell to the ground.

"What?!" the leader exclaimed.

A loud roar descended from above, and a giant shadow spread across the ground. Tom looked up to spot a massive bird, eclipsing the sun and belching bullets like a fiery dragon. It was a Russian attack helicopter—a Hind.

"What?" the leader asked again in disbelief.

"Helicopter!" the executioner shouted.

A blast from the helo ripped into the executioner and knocked him against Tom, slamming them both to the earth.

"Run!" the leader shouted. He and his men scattered like cockroaches.

Tom pocketed his pick and promptly swiped the executioner's ax from his hands. The brown handle was colored like wood, but it felt light and smooth, like high-impact plastic. Tom was an expert with bladed weapons, but this was the largest he'd wielded in combat. His father often shared his Marine Corps mantra: "Improvise, adapt, overcome." Tom rose to his feet and sprinted for the space between the two closest buildings.

Long Beard ran beside him. *Whoosh.* A rocket flew down from the Hind. *Boom!* Another detonation rocked the ground, blowing Tom and Long Beard spout over teakettle. Tom fought to his feet, pleased that he'd held on to the ax. He helped Long Beard up, and they raced away from the hovering beast.

Another explosion sounded, quaking the ground, and fragments flew from the building to the left. Tom pivoted to the adobe brick building to his right and burst inside. Long Beard tumbled in after him.

They were in the living room of someone's house. Tom looked at Long Beard's handcuffs and remembered he had a pick. He removed it from his pocket, pointed it at the handcuffs, and said in Arabic, "I can open those."

Long Beard seemed surprised that Tom could speak his language. "Please."

Tom set down his ax and went to work on the lock. This time was easier than when he had to unlock his own. Long Beard's handcuffs came undone and fell to the ground. He smiled.

Boom! The floor rumbled, and one wall heaved before falling apart and creating a gaping, ragged hole. Through a cloud of dust, Tom could see that other buildings were reduced to rubble. The Hind continued to spit death. Black-clad men shouted and cried out as they ran chaotically. One lifted an RPG and fired off a rocket at the Hind, but the helo answered with bullets from a Yak-B Gatling gun, literally cutting the man down. Tom's building caught on fire, so he picked up his ax and said, "Time to go."

Tom exited the building first and turned. Smack in front of him was the Daesh leader, but now his eyes were mongo. Tom let bygones be bygones and buried the hatchet—at a forty-five degree angle between the leader's shoulder and neck, busting through bone and life fluid. Tom's call sign wasn't Tomahawk for nothing. The leader folded sideways like a paper fan. Tom picked up his AK and handed the ax to Long Beard.

On the road ahead of them was a rusted, bullet-riddled sports car with the windshield blown out and the driver kicked back like he was lost in a daydream. Tom aimed at him while approaching the vehicle, calling to Long Beard, "Watch my back."

"You're American, aren't you?" Long Beard asked.

Tom ignored his question and carefully opened the car door.

"We're on the same side," Long Beard said with the first hint of optimism in his deep voice.

Tom glanced over his shoulder to make sure Long Beard was guarding their rear. He was. Then Tom returned his attention to the man in the car. His face looked like a sledgehammer had slammed through it, and he wore black like the other Daesh terrorists, but this jihadi's fanatical days were over.

There was wet goo all over the interior of the vehicle, most of it concentrated in the driver's seat. Tom removed the body and sat in a puddle. The blood on the floorboard was slick like motor oil. He propped the leader's AK between his legs with the barrel facing down.

He noticed the key in the ignition. With the noise of the Hind and people running for cover or shooting back, Tom hadn't heard the sports car's engine running, but now he could clearly hear it. "Let's go!" Tom called out to Long Beard.

Long Beard turned.

Crack!

The top of Long Beard's head split open like a canoe rack, and he dropped face first.

Tom didn't know the source of the shooter, and he didn't stick around to find out. He put the car in drive and gunned the accelerator. He'd hoped to drop off Long Beard at his destination, exchange quick words, and part ways, but that wasn't meant to be. Now Tom had to get out of the kill zone—fast! And find his brother Max.

Chapter Ten

"*Es-hy*," a man's voice said in Arabic. Wake up. "Es-hy..."

Max slowly forced his eyelids open. He lay on a floor blurry-eyed, staring down a long, thin, beige line, one of many, divided by toasted yellow squares that created long beige rectangles on the carpet. Between the thin beige lines were thick cinnamon lines and an occasional bar made up of beige, toasted yellow, and cinnamon triangles. It reminded him of lines on a carpet in a mosque, where Muslims lined up for prayer. This place was spacious enough for a hundred worshippers. The neatness of the lines was disrupted by nearly a hundred books strewn about—Qurans.

A hand gave him a shake. "Es-hy."

Max blinked the sleepy out of his eyes and turned to the sound of the voice. A grandfatherly man with a white beard and wearing a white flowing robe stood above him. He had the aura of a holy man—an imam. Behind him was a microphone for the call to prayer and an arched doorway bordered with artful geometric patterns. Natural light shone down from high windows and artificial light came from a chandelier. Max sat up unsteadily. "How'd I get here?"

The imam had a Quran in hand, and he picked up another. His Arabic was kind: "When I came in this morning, I found you here. I don't know how you got here." He pointed at the scattered Qurans. "This is not good. We need to pick up Allah's word."

A middle-aged man in a white robe entered the room and promptly pitched in. They were the only ones here.

The last thing Max remembered was visiting a restaurant named Al Azal with his brother to grab a bite to eat and possibly gather some intel. "Was there anyone else with me this morning?"

The imam picked up another Quran. "Yes." He pointed to the other books on the floor. "Please."

Max reached out, grabbed the nearest Quran, and stood with it. He wobbled at first, but he didn't fall over. He put the book on one of the small book nooks located throughout the mosque, and he proceeded toward another Quran. He walked past it and headed for the exit.

The imam called after him, "Aren't you going to help?"

"When I come back." Max opened the door. He didn't give a squirrel's nut about the imam, his mosque, or Allah's word, and he had no intention of returning. He only wanted to find out what happened to his brother.

"Say hello to your fiancé."

The door closed behind Max. *What?* He wasn't engaged.

Outside, Max recognized the Anti-Lebanon Mountains in the distance, rising ten thousand feet in the air. He wasn't entirely sure, but he still had to be in Damascus. He used the mountains to orient himself. He walked to an intersection with intermittent traffic that ran north, south, east, and west. These particular streets didn't look familiar. He pulled out his smartphone to check his map, but his battery was dead.

His gut told him to go south, so he did, hoping to jog his memory. If he could find last night's restaurant or his safe house, he had a better chance of finding Tom. The road was ashen, and he passed a block that had been reduced to rubble. For a capital city, there weren't many people out and about. Maybe he wasn't in Damascus. A pair of young men with dead expressions carried red plastic fuel containers. It was like walking through the remains of an apocalypse. Max touched his abdomen—his Glock was still there in a concealed holster, ready to smoke check any zombies that happened his way. He tapped his pocket, and his apartment and car keys jingled. Also attached to his keyring was a mini red flashlight. *Good.*

Then he noticed something on his ring finger that wasn't there before—a gold ring. *Jewelry?* He felt his ear lobes for earrings and was thankful when he discovered none.

Gunfire rattled in the distance behind him, but it was too far away to worry about. After three hundred meters, he came to a shop with a sign that read "Home Goods" in Arabic. *This seems strangely familiar.* At the crossroad he turned west and spotted a grocery store that he thought he'd seen before. He eyed the Al Azal restaurant up ahead.

He was still in Jobar, an eastern district in Damascus, where the medieval Jewish synagogue had stood until 2014, when it was destroyed by civil war bombing and looting. Now Syrian government and rebel forces battled for control of the neighborhood.

Max had just crossed the parking lot of Al Azal when a one-legged man on the opposite side of the lot crossed over to Max's side and said, "Thief, you stole my goat."

"I didn't steal your goat," Max said.

The one-legged man flared his nostrils. "Last night, you stole my goat!"

"I didn't steal your goat, but I'll help you find it." It was true that Max hadn't stolen the goat, or at least he thought he hadn't, but he wasn't going to help the man find it. He had more important things to do—he had to find his brother.

The man raised his fist in anger and shook it.

Max was still a bit woozy, and he staggered through the front door of Al Azal. The hay-like fragrance of saffron was thick, and black pepper tickled his sinuses. He recognized the rustic interior and jukebox from the previous night, like a familiar biker bar. He and Tom had posed as French journalists and eaten dinner at the table in the far corner. It wasn't lunchtime yet, and the place was quiet except for a woman wearing walloping big hair, heavy makeup, bright colors, high heels, and bling from head to toe. She chatted anxiously with a young woman at the cash register. The cashier pointed at Max, and Bling turned to face him.

Max became agitated, as if he'd just sailed into the eye of a storm. He stuck with his cover as a French journalist and asked the cashier, "Have you seen a French guy in here, a little taller than me and with longer hair?"

The cashier's eyes evaded him. "No."

Bling chattered excitedly: "You must pay me the rest of the money for the engagement rings."

"I didn't buy any engagement rings," Max said.

She aimed her finger at the ring on Max's finger, as if she was trying to shoot it off.

Max took the gold ring off and gave it to her. "Keep it."

Bling spoke in a loud, pneumatic tone. "I can't take back a used ring. And your fiancé has the other one."

Max was still confused about what in the hell was going on, but he was able to think on his feet. "The engagement is off—you collect the ring from her!" He stormed past her into the kitchen, now beginning to suspect that maybe he and his brother had been drugged. A cook with the word *shahada*, or faith, tattooed in Arabic script on one of his thick forearms froze midway into chopping parsley and stared at him like he'd seen the devil. Max searched a storage area and inside a large freezer. Nada. He felt like a conspiracy nut waving a gun in a pizzeria and looking for kidnapped children who weren't there.

He returned to the main part of the restaurant, where Bling gave him a wide berth.

A waitress asked, "Would you like a table?"

"Look, I don't know who drugged me last night or what happened, but my restaurant review is going to say that your food ain't memorable!" Max threw open the front door and blew out.

In the parking lot, he was relieved not to see the one-legged man with the missing goat. Even so, he wished a curse on the restaurant: *You shifty-eyed sons of bitches drugged my brother and me, and who knows what in the world happened to him. Of all the things in the world you could take from me, you better not have taken my brother, or I will return with a fuel tanker truck and a flamethrower and rain unholy hell down on this neighborhood.*

He decided to head back to an apartment leased from a local CIA asset to see if his brother had shown up there, but first he had to make sure he wasn't followed and that no one saw him coming. He marched through the weeds between a puke-green apartment building and a mangled wire fence. High-spirited talking, cartoonish sound effects, and applause came from the apartment, like noise from a TV game show. Max poked his head around the corner to see if it was clear. It was. He crept through the backyard. More cautious now, he approached within fifty meters of the safe house.

He sneaked through a hole in a concrete wall and glanced back to see if anyone had followed him. No one had. Between the wall with the hole in it and his safe house, the ground was sandy with some weeds poking up—little in the way of cover and concealment, so he picked up the pace to limit his exposure. He panned the open area—clear—and he bounded over the next wall. He landed behind a two-story tan building where the safe house was located and entered. He looked for signs of surveillance, but saw none. Then he climbed the stairs to the second floor.

Outside his front door, Max listened for a moment. Children played nearby and a young woman talked to them, but no sound came from inside his apartment. He slipped the key in the hole carefully and turned it slowly so as not to make noise. He took a deep breath. Then he drew his pistol and opened the door. He rushed inside.

It was a small two-bedroom apartment, and there was no one in the living room. He hurried past books on a small bookshelf and looked in the kitchen. Hungry, he wanted to grab something out of the fridge, but that would have to wait until he finished making sure the safe house was safe. He checked the other rooms but found nothing out of place. The door to the bathroom was shut, and he hadn't checked it yet. From inside came sounds, like the steps of someone wearing hard-soled shoes or boots. Max aimed at the door. He would first have to identify who was inside so he didn't end up shooting his brother. If it was an armed threat, Max would have to get off the first shot before his opponent did.

His heart rate pumped up and his palms became wet. Max took a deep breath to steady his nerves, and he gripped his pistol tighter so it wouldn't slip out of his hands. Realizing he was gripping it too tightly, which could throw off his aim, he loosened up a little.

The toilet flushed. *That has to be Tom. Or it could be an insurgent. Maybe this is a terrorist who's been waiting a long time and couldn't wait any more to relieve himself.* The footsteps sounded again—then a knock on the door. Max aimed and anticipated the door opening. But it didn't. *Is he playing with me?*

Max couldn't stand the suspense any longer. He flung open the door and pointed his muzzle inside. A brown figure stared at him—a goat.

Max stared at it: "Seriously?"

The goat took a step back. Max did, too. Then it charged. Its head planted in Max's crotch and knocked him on his ass. Max's head flushed white hot, and the room twisted around in circles. The air whooshed out of his lungs, and he'd lost most of his strength, but he retained his pistol. He struggled to his feet and tried to catch his breath. His stomach churned as if it was about to hurl chunks.

The goat backed up again, stamped the deck, lowered its head and shoulders, and curved its neck.

"Oh, no!" Max said.

The goat charged, but this time Max sidestepped it, and the animal missed him. Max considered shooting it, but decided against the noise.

He holstered his pistol and hopped on the menace, forcing it into submission. Then he dragged it out the front door, shoved it into the hall, and slammed the door.

Still nauseous and a bit loopy, he did remember that his phone needed charging, so he found an electrical outlet in the living room and plugged in his charger and phone. Electricity often went out in Damascus, but now his phone lit up.

The doorknob to the front door jiggled.

Max drew his Glock and aimed. He figured it was probably that troublesome goat, but he was prepared just in case it wasn't.

A tall guy entered the doorway and aimed in Max's direction.

"Tommy!" Max grinned.

Tom smiled, too. "Max!"

"You okay?"

"Barely," Tom said. "You?"

"Somebody drugged me, and I did some crazy-ass shit I don't remember. And a goat head-butted me in the family jewels. Other than that, I'm fine."

Tom shook his head. "The goat outside our door?"

"It's evil."

"Someone drugged me, too," Tom said. "And Daesh kidnapped me."

"Holy shit—I'm glad you made it back."

"I was hoping I'd find you here, too."

"You clean?" Max asked.

"Probably not. You?"

"It's like they knew we were here from the moment we arrived. Now I seem to remember you dancing like a fool with your shirt off, and me cheering you on."

"That's more than I remember." Tom walked over to the refrigerator and opened it.

Max dropped his keister on a stuffed chair next to his charging phone, picked the phone up, and accessed a hidden app for texting their boss, Willy. He typed a brief SITREP, reporting their situation.

Tom fetched an apple, sat down on the couch, and bit into the red fruit. "We should get our blood and urine tested."

The United States no longer had an embassy in Syria, but the Czech Republic did, and they let America run a US Interests Section, mainly for emergencies. The Czech Republic Embassy was only a twenty-minute ride west. In contrast, the closest American embassy was in Amman, Jordan, a three-hour drive south. "Let's go to the Czech embassy." Max's phone wasn't finished charging, but he finished typing his SITREP and added: Let the US Interests Section at the Czech Embassy know we're coming. Then he tapped SEND.

Chapter Eleven

Unlike Cain, who killed his brother Abel, Max *was* his brother's keeper, and he watched him for signs of poisoning as they descended the stairs. Tom's face wasn't pale or red, and he didn't miss a step as they parted with the safe house and goat.

"What?" Tom asked.

"Nothing."

At the ground floor, Max bounded over the back wall, his brother at his side. They dashed across the sand and clumps of weeds. The hole in the wall was a good ambush spot—or bad ambushee spot, depending on one's perspective. Max crept carefully through the hole to the other side. Then he slipped into the parking lot of the puke-green apartment building.

"Daesh took my *pistolet* and phone," Tom said, "but I can drive."

Max reached in his pocket, grabbed the keys, and tossed them to Tom.

They hopped into a gray Kia Sorrento SUV—its bullet-resistant windows and body, blast-resistant floorboard, and fake patches of rust courtesy of the Agency. The truck came alive with a growl and leaped forward.

Max wanted to smoke check any zombies, so he drew his pistol and held it in his lap. Low-viz ops such as this often traded off the heavier firepower of assault rifles for the concealability of compact pistols, but now that the enemy seemed to know of their presence, concealability was as useful as an ejection seat on a helicopter. On top of that, Tom was down a pistol. "Wish we had our M4s," Max said.

"Ditto." Tom drove into Zombieland. They passed a row of five-story buildings whose fronts and tops had been ripped off, the exposed rooms hollowed out and blackened. Whole corners of buildings sagged as if a giant had jumped on them, leaving only the middles standing tall. Beside one of the buildings rested a black BMW with two men in it. It was the only vehicle in this ghostly neighborhood except for Max and Tom's.

Max and Tom rolled by a Leaning Tower of Pisa and a building flattened like a stack of tortillas. Max glanced back to see if the BMW followed, but it didn't. *Maybe it's nothing.*

They rode past a mosque with a five-story minaret posted above a four-story base, nine stories in all. The tip-top of the structure was gone, and only the vertical shaft of the minaret remained. A ten-foot-long rectangular wall of the minaret seemingly floated in midair, clinging to nearly invisible threads of steel. The four stories at the base of the mosque were pockmarked with holes big and small.

He checked behind again. "We've got company—black BMW." It kept its distance—not too far, not too close.

Tom looked in his rearview mirror. "I see it."

"Let's find out if they're following us."

Tom turned right. The BMW did, too—not too fast, not too slow. "Once could be a coincidence," Tom said.

Tom turned right again—so did the BMW. "Twice is no coincidence," Max said.

"Maybe they know who drugged us last night," Tom said.

"Let's ask them."

Tom made another right, and after the turn, he sped off the road and parked beside the crumbled concrete of a caved-in structure. There they hid. The BMW cruised past.

Tom backed out of hiding and followed them surreptitiously.

Max slapped the dashboard. "Surprise, bitches." He looked over at Tom and saw he had his seatbelt on, and now seemed an appropriate time, so Max buckled up, too.

The BMW maintained its cool, like its occupants didn't care that they were being followed. Abruptly the car turned right and took off like a hawk out of hell. *They do care.*

Max and Tom gave chase. Tom sped past the same apocalypse row, Tower of Pisa, and mosque with the floating wall.

The BMW bolted down a debris-strewn street, dodging chunks of building and a trash dumpster that was in the wrong place at the wrong time. Tom dodged them, too. Then they picked up speed—scrotum-shrinkingly faster.

The BMW swerved into a turn. Its smoking tires laid down black streaks on the dusty pavement and screeched. Tom overshot the turn. The burned-out concrete frame of a building grew large, and Max thought, *So this is how it ends—taken out by an inanimate object. This is so embarrassing.*

Tom let off the gas and pumped the brakes, but their momentum took them up on the sidewalk and directly at the building. Concrete rocks and pebbles slid beneath them, but Tom regained control and narrowly missed hitting the edifice.

The engine growled, and the SUV leaped off the sidewalk. Ahead, the BMW had slowed down, and Max and Tom gained on it. The vehicle swerved as the passenger hung his weapon out the window and sprayed AK fire.

Bullets struck the front of their SUV, and one hit the windshield in front of Max's face. Max's heart and breathing stopped. In that moment, the whole world froze. Then he remembered the bullet-resistant glass and realized he hadn't been hit. His heart pumped again and he could breathe. Another bullet struck the window between them and one hit above Tom. The shooter continued fire until he'd spent his magazine.

Max rolled down his passenger window. "My turn."

Tom pulled up on the BMWs left side. Max blasted at the driver, a little man who cowered and scrunched down in his seat while keeping the BMW on the road. Max's shots missed. The gunman in the passenger seat presented a bigger target, so Max fired at him. The shoulder fabric on his shirt twitched—direct hit. It wasn't a killing shot, but it had gotten his attention. Max aimed at his face and squeezed. The shooter's head smacked sideways like a cue ball and bounced off the passenger window.

Tom sideswiped the BMW and ran it off the road. The vehicle skidded out of control until it hit the concrete structure of a burned-out building, stopping the car cold.

Tom slammed on the brakes, sliding to a stop. Then he backed up and parked on the side of the road next to the BMW. Its front was smashed. Max wanted to interrogate the driver, and he wasted no time as he hopped out and ran to the Bimmer. In the passenger seat was the shooter, his piñata popped and his candy leaking onto the leather upholstery. The driver's airbag was deployed and bloodied, and the small man's head seemed buried in it, but upon closer inspection, his head was on the floorboard. The airbag seemed to have decapitated him.

Chapter Twelve

Contrasting the apocalypse that was eastern Damascus, Tom drove with Max through paradise—palm tree–lined streets, embassies, and bank headquarters—in western Damascus. The Papal Embassy, Saudi Arabia Embassy, Al Baraka Islamic Bank, and International Committee of the Red Cross surrounded the Czech Republic Embassy.

Tom parked, and he and his brother strolled into the Czech embassy as if they belonged there.

A young clerk on the other side of the counter looked down his nose at them. Behind him was a large office area and more rooms where his coworkers shuffled papers, typed, and answered phones.

"We need to talk to the US Interests Section," Max said. "They're expecting us."

"Please," Tom added.

The clerk spoke English in the monotone of a machine gun, and he pronounced *z* instead of *th*: "You should not be in Damascus—zere is a civil war going on here."

"Like you, we have business here," Tom said kindly. He was the negotiator; Max was the fighter.

"You're not like me," the clerk said, puffing out his chest proudly.

Max repeated: "We need to talk to the US Interests Section. They're expecting us."

"Zat's only for emergencies," the diplomat said.

"This is an emergency," Tom said.

"Vat kind of emergency?"

Max fantasized breaking the clerk's bones. "Medical."

"Zen you should go to zee hospital."

"Can I speak to your supervisor?" Max interjected.

The clerk paused as if surprised. "Vun moment, please." Then he slunk away.

When the clerk was out of earshot, Max did Steve Martin's Czech swinger impression: "You Americans are so naive. When you break up wiz a girl, you make such a big deal. Where I'm from, our way to break up is simple and mature. We tell zee girl, 'I break wiz zee, I break wiz zee, I break wiz zee.' Zen we toss dog poo on her shoe. Later, my brozer and I, we go to zee crazy singles bar, and we look for zee girls wiz zee dog poo on zeir shoes."

Tom rolled his eyes. "Dude."

Max grinned. He turned and spotted a leggy brunette with her ID pinned on her blouse and a frown on her face. She stood on the visitor's side of the counter, waiting to access the staff area. "*Ahoj*," he greeted her in Czech.

She wasn't impressed. "Yeah," she said in English. An electrical buzz sounded, a metal door opened, and she passed over to the staff side of the counter. Then the door closed and the heavy metallic click of a lock sounded.

Max wanted to relax for a moment, but he knew that if he sat down he might be forgotten, so he remained standing to let the embassy staff know he was still waiting for help.

Minutes later, a confident man arrived and said in perfect English, "Sorry to have kept you waiting. My name is Gus. Could I see some ID, please?"

Max and Tom showed him their French passports.

Gus opened the passports and studied them. "Our friend Willy said you'd be coming. I'll take you to the nurse."

Max nodded.

"Thank you," Tom said.

Gus pointed to the door to the side, and Max and his brother walked over and stopped in front of it. The buzzing sounded, the lock clicked, and the door opened. Max and Tom walked through. It clicked shut behind them.

Gus led them through the office area to a restroom. He pointed inside, getting right down to business. "The collection containers for the urine samples are in there."

Tom walked in first. Max waited and Gus stood by. Then Tom came out with his sample. "Only two-thirds full?" Max asked.

"Is it a contest?" Tom asked.

Max went inside. On the container was a label and next to it was a Sharpie pen. He wrote his cover name on the label and his cover birth date. Then he filled the container to the rim. He proudly exited the bathroom with his full container.

Gus escorted him around the corner to a small room, where his brother was giving his blood sample. In the room was a bunk bed, cabinets and drawers, a small refrigerator, some boxes on the floor, a stethoscope and ear probe on a desk, weight scale, stretcher standing in the corner, and other medical equipment. The office had a familiar sanitary smell that Max didn't care for. He preferred to stay out of hospitals and medical offices—he preferred to live among the healthy.

The nurse taking Tom's blood was the same leggy brunette who'd frowned at Max earlier. He read her nametag: Ladislava Prochazka. She glared at Max, who smiled at her sheepishly. He tried to make nice and told a fib: "Ladislava is a pretty name."

She gestured to the counter next to the sink, where Tom's urine sample sat. Max put his sample next to his brother's.

She bandaged Tom's arm, and he stood up and stepped to the side. Max sat on the stool beside the nurse. Nurse Prochazka cleaned a spot on his arm with an alcohol pad—so far, so good. Then she poked his arm with the needle. She missed the vein. The needle stung, but Max kept his mouth shut. She pulled it out and inserted again. Another miss. This time Max blurted out, "Ouch!" He glanced at Tom, who seemed concerned. Max wondered how many more times she could screw this up. *Probably a lot.*

Without emotion, she readied the needle to stick him again. "I really thought your Czech impression was hilarious. What a gift you have."

He realized that this was punishment. Max gave in and tried to make peace. "No, it wasn't funny, not at all."

She poked him with the needle. This time the needle hit the vein, and blood trickled into the vial. When she finished drawing his blood, she put a small bandage on his wound and gave a big smile. "Have a nice day."

"Thank you," Max said politely, hoping he wouldn't have to get poked by her again.

The quiet of the small medical office was suddenly broken by a shriek that rang out from somewhere in the embassy, followed by panicked voices. Instinctively Max's left hand snapped to his belly. He grasped his shirt and pulled it up. Simultaneously, his right hand shot to his pistol grip. He wanted to be ready but he didn't know the seriousness of the threat, so he maintained his grip on his weapon but kept it in its abdomen holster. He let his shirt fall to partially conceal the pistol and used his free hand to further conceal his weapon. *What the hell?*

Tom reacted similarly for his gun that wasn't there. Then his face looked like he'd sucked on a lemon.

Max cracked open the door to investigate. The proud young clerk and Gus helped a middle-aged Caucasian man stagger down the hall toward Max. Blood dripped on the linoleum between the man's feet, leaving a crimson trail behind, and his blood-covered hands clutched his gut as if holding his entrails in. He rambled in Czech as if in shock, begging for help.

There seemed to be no immediate threats in the vicinity. Max released his weapon and opened the door wide for the wounded man. "*Chirurg*," the wounded man cried. "Chirurg, Chirurg."

Nurse Prochazka immediately grabbed a stretcher and laid it on the deck. Max and the others helped lay the man on his back on the stretcher. He quieted down a bit, and Max raised the man's knees to lessen the pain and control for shock.

Nurse Prochazka whipped out a large bandage. Max, Tom, and the others backed away to give her room to work. She removed the man's hands from his wound and applied the white side of the bandage to the injury.

"Explosion?" Max asked.

Nurse Prochazka slipped the tail of the bandage under the man, brought it up around his other side, and tied it—tight enough to keep it in place, but not so tight as to cause more damage to his organs. "No explosion," she said. "Incision was too neat, like he was cut open with a scalpel. We must take him to the hospital—I need all four of you to help carry him."

Max, Tom, Gus, and the young clerk took their places on each handle of the stretcher.

"Lift him on three," she said. "One, two, three."

They hoisted the casualty in unison. Others had gathered at the doorway, but now they made a space. Nurse Prochazka led Max and the other stretcher bearers through the embassy. She called out in Czech and recruited more help. Outside, they put the wounded man in the back of a black four-wheel-drive Land Rover.

She turned to Max and said, "We've got it from here, thank you." She loaded into the Land Rover with her newly formed posse and sped away.

Gus escorted Max and Tom along the blood trail back into the embassy.

"Who was the wounded man?" Max asked.

Gus led them into his office. "His name is Honza Novák. He's a Czech diplomat."

"He said 'chirurg,'" Tom said. "What does that mean?"

Gus locked the door and sat down behind his desk. "Surgeon."

"He asked for a surgeon?" Tom said.

"No. There's a Syrian man called the Surgeon. He kidnaps people, removes organs, and sells them on the black market, sharing the profit with the Syrian government. Until now he only did this to anti-government rebels. There have been rumors that he performs experiments on regular civilians, too, but we don't know much more."

Max cracked his knuckles. "Some doctor."

"We might've heard of him," Tom said.

"Nurse Prochazka mentioned that the incision on Honza was clean," Gus said. "That is consistent with his mode of operation."

"Do you have any more information on the Surgeon?" Max asked.

"Still working on it." Gus pulled open his desk drawer and produced a smartphone, a Czech CZ 75 compact pistol, two magazines, a hip holster, and magazine pouches. He handed them to Tom. "Willy said you'd be needing these. The phone is an older model, but it's the best I could come up with on short notice."

"Where'd you get the pistol?" Tom asked.

Gus smiled. "It was a gift. But I'm sure you'll put it to good use."

Tom took off his belt and attached the holster and magazine pouches. "Thank you."

"Yeah, thanks," Max said.

"We'll fly the urine and blood samples to Landstuhl Regional Medical Center in Germany for analysis," Gus said. "Willy will let you know the results. Is there anything else?"

Tom buckled his belt, press checked his pistol to make sure it was loaded, and holstered it. His shirt was long enough to cover everything, so he was good. "No, you've been more than helpful."

Max's phone rang. He answered, "What's up?"

A voice answered in Arabic; it was the Syrian militiaman who'd helped Max kill the Russian sniper. "It's Sami. I found the location of Hospital 175, where the Surgeon does his work. I'll text you the address and floor plan, and I'm attaching his photo. I figured Azrael would tell me to get it, so I did."

Max remembered Azrael, his reggae music, and the video of Saddam Hussein. "Why isn't Azrael calling me?"

"I thought you knew. Azrael is dead."

"Dead?"

"His throat was slit. And the other things they did to him... they are unspeakable."

"Who did it?" Max asked.

"The Russians. You killed their sniper; now they want revenge. What they did to Azrael—if they could do that to the angel of death, imagine what they could do to you or me. I'm sorry, I've got to go. We're all worried for our safety now." Sami hung up.

Max checked Sami's message. In it was the address of Hospital 175. He opened the document with the hospital's floor plan. *Good.* Then he opened an unlabeled JPG. The photo of the surgeon showed a slim, elderly man with silver hair, wrinkled skin, and his nose up in the air. *Great.*

Chapter Thirteen

In a dark operating room of Hospital 175, the Surgeon studied a hooded prisoner as two orderlies brought him in limping. The Surgeon nodded, and the orderlies removed the man's hood. The doctor presented himself as well spoken and polite: "Hello. The warden said that you complained about your leg."

"Y-yes. I think it's a sprain," the prisoner said.

The Surgeon examined his injured leg more closely. "Hmm." He turned to the orderlies. "Strap him to the table. For his own safety."

The prisoner panicked and tried to push the orderlies away, but he was malnourished and weak, and the orderlies manhandled him onto an old, stained wooden table. There was a drain below it in the floor to take away any body fluids. The prisoner tried to kick and flail, but the orderlies secured his arms and legs with leather straps, followed by his head. Finally, they bound his stomach.

"It's just a sprain," the prisoner pleaded. "There's no need for... this."

The Surgeon put on a pair of gloves. Then he went behind the prisoner and retrieved a sledgehammer from the corner. He'd tried an ordinary claw hammer before, but its force was concentrated in too small an area for his taste.

The Surgeon liked surprises, but he liked suspense, too. He remained standing behind the prisoner and stared at him. The prisoner's lips trembled, and the trembling spread to his chin and throughout his whole body. The Surgeon waited for him to close his eyes. He did. And the Surgeon waited some more.

Then he moved in close and heaved the sledgehammer up. He was in his sixties, and it took much of his strength, but he knew that the higher he raised it, the harder the large, heavy, metal head would come down—with little or no effort on his own part. At first the head rose swiftly, but its rise decelerated rapidly, and his arm muscles strained to hoist it every last centimeter. He put his back and legs into it and strained until the tool reached its maximum height. At its zenith, gravity took over, relieving him of the burden. The head came down, slowly at first but accelerating rapidly until it reached brutal velocity and smashed into the prisoner's leg.

"Owhee!" he wailed.

The Surgeon broke a sweat as he rested the sledgehammer's head on the floor with the handle sticking up. "It's not a sprain—it's broken."

The prisoner cried, "Why?"

"You're an enemy of the state," the Surgeon said. "I'm told that you clicked Like on some subversive posts."

"My only crime was clicking Like on a nonpolitical post by an acquaintance who was anti-government."

"I'm a doctor, not a politician." The Surgeon examined the man's leg again. "This looks quite bad. I'm afraid we'll have to amputate." The Surgeon walked around behind the prisoner again.

"No, no, no!"

This time, the Surgeon retrieved his bone saw and returned to the front of his patient. He stood there for a moment so the man could more fully appreciate what was about to happen.

Sweat and tears streamed down the patient's face, and every part of his body appeared to fight the restraints, but he couldn't stop the inevitable. His breathing became rapid and shallow and his voice rose in a shrill: "Please, please, pleeease!"

The Surgeon put on his mask. "I'll be gentle. This won't hurt a bit. I promise."

The prisoner hyperventilated.

The Surgeon sawed through the soft flesh until he hit the hard leg bone—and he kept sawing, focused like a laser beam. He enjoyed the dry, metallic smell of the prisoner's blood and the music of the fluids hitting the floor, but he didn't let his enjoyment get in the way of his concentration.

The prisoner screamed.

Both of the orderlies looked away.

The saw moved freely now. The Surgeon had cut completely through the other side of the leg and struck the table. He set down his saw, unfastened two leather straps, picked up the amputated leg, and marveled at his handiwork.

The prisoner could not share in the viewing because he had passed out.

Chapter Fourteen

The night extinguished the sun, and Max sat in the passenger side as Tom parked their SUV among a handful of vehicles on the north side of Hospital 175. Max had dressed like a doctor, wearing a white smock that concealed his *pistolet*. He carried an empty stuff bag attached to a D-ring on his belt. Tom was dressed the same.

Two doctors exited the building, gesturing and conversing with each other.

Max and his brother stayed in their vehicle until the doctors loaded into their cars and drove away. The brothers unassed the Kia and jogged to the door. Tom stood guard while Max turned the knob. He hoped lady luck would smile on him, and it would be unlocked. It was locked. *Damn.*

Max pulled out an L-shaped Quiet Steel tension wrench and pick. He inserted the small end of the wrench into the lock and turned until it stopped. Then he poked the pick inside the top of the keyhole. At the end of the pick was a hook that he used to lift the first spring-loaded pin inside the lock. He rotated the wrench, but he didn't maintain enough pressure on the first pin and it fell back into place, so he had to start over. He lifted the first spring again, but this time he deftly rotated the wrench to maintain pressure on the first pin, keeping it up. Now he couldn't get the second pin up, so he had to ease off on the pressure until it rose. One by one he lifted each remaining pin with the pick and kept it up with tension from the wrench. Deeper and deeper he probed and manipulated the lock until the final pin surrendered. He turned the wrench once more, and the door unlocked. He wiped the perspiration from his brow and pocketed his lock pick tools. Success felt good.

Max opened the door a crack and peeked inside. He was at the end of a long, brightly lit hall. No one was in sight. He didn't have to signal his brother with fancy military or ninja signals—Tom knew what to do. They were big boys playing by big boy rules.

Max hustled into the hall. He'd only gone a few meters when a pair of doctors entered the hall, too. Max's heart jolted, and he snatched the nearest door handle. *Unlocked.* He didn't have time to rejoice. He ducked inside. The room was dark, and Tom joined him.

Max's breathing became heavy, and his heart raced. Arabic voices from out in the hall were muffled and indistinct—coming closer. Footsteps became louder.

Max's mother's voice came to him. She'd been a photogenic Parisian who died much too young. When he got nervous, she told him in French, "*Prends une grande respiration.*" Take a deep breath.

He did. Each breath brought him bliss, and his nerves settled down. The voices and footsteps reached their crescendo before they faded. Max peeked out. Once again, the hall was clear. He raced out of the room to the nearest stairs and down into the basement. The lights were off here. He reached into his pocket, pulled out his keyring, and switched on his mini red flashlight to see where he was going. Max snuck through the basement area until he reached an office. On the floor plan he'd studied earlier, this room was supposed to be the Surgeon's office, which led to his operating room. He crept past a coat rack and stuffed leather sofa. Against one wall, a bookshelf was filled with thick books in English and Arabic. On the desk was a notebook, a computer, and several thumb drives. Max scooped up the notebook and put it in the intel bag linked to his belt. Then he stuffed the thumb drives in his pockets.

While Max stuffed his intel bag, Tom fired up the PC to bypass the password and hack the computer. Something was wrong. Tom shook his head. He couldn't get in.

C'est la vie. Such is life.

Max cautiously approached the door leading to the surgery room. He opened it slightly and looked and listened. It was too dark to see, but he could hear a dripping sound. He shined his flashlight inside.

On a wall were faded photos that appeared to be of various stages of medical operations. In the middle of the room was a primitive wooden operating table, and on it was a man's body. Beside him was a dolly with trays containing a scalpel and other tools. Max checked the man for signs of life, but there were none. His leg was missing, and blood painted the table and floor. *Poor bastard.*

On a low table was a *safarta*, an Arab lunch box made of three stacked bowls. Max undid the side latch and examined the top bowl. Empty. He checked out the next bowl. It was empty, too. He dreaded what he'd find in the bottom tier, but he looked inside anyway. There he found a bowl of half-eaten rice.

Tom opened a small refrigerator and removed an aluminum vial. He mouthed a silent gasp and showed the vial to Max. It was marked: BK-16. Tom opened the refrigerator door wide so Max could see inside. There were more vials with the same markings.

Tom grinned hard.

Max did, too. *Finally!* He wanted to cheer out loud, but they weren't out of danger yet, so he did a quick fist pump. Then he took the safarta to the freezer, pulled out some ice, and packed it in one of the bowls. He handed Tom the bowl and signaled him to put the vials in it—Max would stand guard while Tom gathered the BK-16.

A door opened, and a light came on in the office/waiting area outside the operating room. Tom still had more vials to pack.

Footsteps followed. Max turned off his red light, drew his Glock, and posted himself next to the door to the surgery room. With the flick of a switch, Max shifted from foraging mode to hunting mode.

More footsteps came. Now it sounded like two to three men. The footsteps became louder, closer. Tom stuffed vials into another bowl, but he still had to close the contraption. Their only way out was through the office. *We're trapped.*

The light came on in the operating room, temporarily blinding Max. He quickly recognized the old man from the picture that Azrael sent—the Surgeon—who was flanked by two armed Syrian military men, one with longish hair and the other with short hair. Max aimed at Long Hair and popped two rounds into his chest, knocking him down. Short Hair stepped back and raised his pistol. Max unleashed two rounds to his chest and finished him with one to the head, toppling him like a big domino. Max had fired five shots within a second and a quarter—surprise, speed, and violence were key to winning a gunfight.

Long Hair lay on the deck grabbing his chest and moaning. He was still alive. Max aimed at his head and pressed Mute. His brains leaked onto the floor.

The Surgeon froze. Max pointed his pistol at him and said in Arabic, "Get on the ground—now."

The Surgeon lowered to his knees and held his hands up. Max wanted him prone and didn't waste time with words; instead, he gave the Surgeon a kick to the back, flattening him. "Unngh."

Max bound the man's hands behind his back with flex-cuffs and gagged him.

Tom latched up the safarta with the vials in it. "Let's go."

Max kicked the Surgeon in the crotch to demand his undivided attention. "On your feet."

The Surgeon groaned but moved more quickly this time. Even so, he was too slow. Max shoved him out the door, through the office, out another door, and up the steps.

Max held his pistol down at his side to partially conceal it. Tom did likewise. A nurse and a woman in civilian clothing stopped in the hall and watched them, but Max ignored the pair and escorted the Surgeon the opposite way—the way they'd come in. He didn't like exiting from the same door he'd entered. If enemies had seen them come in, enemies would be waiting for them on their way out. But Max didn't want to exit through the front door or a side entrance and risk being seen by a lot of people. So he chose the lesser of the two evils and hoped an ambush wasn't waiting for them. He pushed the Surgeon through the door, using him as a shield in case they met a hailstorm of bullets. They departed the building.

Except for a handful of parked cars, the lot was clear. Max thrust the Surgeon forward until they reached the Kia. Tom pressed the remote, the doors clicked unlocked, and Max opened the back door, stuffed the Surgeon in, and sat with him.

Tom hopped in front and fired up the engine before spinning out of the parking lot.

Max bagged the Surgeon's head with a black hood. Next, he reached under the seat, pulled out a pair of noise-cancelling headphones, and put them on their captive before cramming him onto the floorboard. The Surgeon groaned, but Max couldn't give a rat's ass about the twisted old man's discomfort.

Tom drove them to the M5 Motorway, the backbone of Syria, and took them out of Damascus. Max texted Willy: hvt secure. They'd captured their high-value target. Max experienced some relief, but they weren't out of the danger zone yet.

He wanted to interrogate the Surgeon now, but he needed to help Tom keep watch for thugs, Daesh, Syrian troops, and other dangers. The interrogation would have to wait until they reached their extract.

<hr/>

TWO HUNDRED MILES OUT of Damascus, Max's phone rang. He looked at the caller ID: Sami. "Hello," Max said in English.

There was no answer.

"Sami?" Max asked.

"Sami cannot come to the phone," an ominous voice said in English.

Max's stomach sank. Sami wasn't a best friend or a tactical genius, but they were on friendly terms, and he delivered good intel. "Who is this?"

"I am the man who is going to kill you."

Max's stomach sank further, but he buoyed it with hubris and levity: "Now why would you say a silly thing like that?"

"You killed one of our men."

"The list is long, buttercup—maybe you can be a bit more specific, jog my memory."

"The sniper in Damascus."

Max swallowed hard. Then he took a moment to swallow normally. "Ah, your Russian buddy. I didn't kill him."

"Then who did?"

"Not who—what. It was the bullet that killed him."

"No matter. I'm going to kill you. And your partner."

Threatening Max was one thing, but threatening his brother made Max's blood boil. He concealed his irritation by piling on more hubris and levity. "I'll come right to your door—just tell me where it is."

The caller ignored Max's sarcasm. "I will meet you in the ring, but I will not throw the fight for you."

"I'd like that," Max said.

"Likewise, I would like that a lot."

"I'll bring a present for you. Just like I gave your comrade."

"You know that is not going to happen. But you know what will happen."

"What name should I put on your present?"

"Put you and your friend's names on it. I'll be quick, I promise."

"You can dream on, fool, but don't waste my time telling me about it. I have not yet begun to fight." Max ended the call, then immediately contacted CIA to trace it.

MAX HAD DRIVEN THE remaining three hundred miles northeast to the outskirts of Kobani, hard on the Turkish border, where the site of a former cement plant owned by France's largest industrial company, Lafarge, was located. When Daesh took control of Syria, Lafarge paid off the terrorists in order to keep on doing business there. Eventually, the payoffs weren't enough, and Daesh commandeered the plant—until American troops and local Kurds arrived and kicked them out. The US transformed it into their forward operating base (FOB) in support of combat and counterterrorist operations in Syria.

The FOB stood like a shadowy apparition in the morning light. HESCO barriers and concertina wire formed a wall around the compound.

"Feels strange coming back here without Dad," Max said.

"I miss him," Tom said.

"Ditto."

Unlike the last time they'd been at the base, the FOB's howitzers weren't booming out artillery shells, and there were no other signs of combat.

A pair of hardened CIA Ground Branch officers in a pickup truck escorted Max, Tom, and the Surgeon to the helo pad.

Max parked near a Chinook helo with its rotor spinning. He left the keys in the ignition and got out of the SUV. "Smells like the stink blowing in from the city has gone, as well."

Tom opened his door, grabbed the Surgeon, and hauled him out like he was a sack of fertilizer. "Can't say I miss the foul odor."

Max helped his brother drag the flex-cuffed Surgeon, who made a guttural sound, to the helo, and they all climbed aboard. Soon the bird lifted off and rose above the FOB's concrete buildings, guard towers, and sandbag-fortified Conex boxes.

Max stood behind their prisoner and watched as Tom removed his noise-reducing headphones, black hood, and gag.

"Help me!" the Surgeon cried out in Arabic.

Tom shouted above the noise of the helo in Arabic: "Up here, no one can here you scream!"

"Is that supposed to scare me?" the Surgeon asked.

"It should," Tom said. "What do you know about BK-16?"

"Nothing," the Surgeon said.

"You don't want to lie to me."

"I'm telling you: nothing."

Tom sighed and stepped back. "If you don't want to tell me..."

Max grabbed a handful of the Surgeon's hair and jerked him onto his back, bouncing his head off the deck. *Bam!*

"Aagh!" the Surgeon yelled. He winced and turned in Max's direction. "Good cop, bad cop—you don't think we have TV in Syria."

Max spoke Arabic, too. "For a smart man, you're not very smart!" He sat the Surgeon upright again. "What do you know about BK-16?"

The Surgeon whined. "My head hurts."

Max didn't like how this piece of shit toyed with lives. He bounced him off the deck again, this time knocking him out.

Seconds later, the Surgeon's eyes opened and he said, "People are going to die."

"What do you know about BK-16?" Max demanded again.

"I just want to go back to being a doctor."

"You're not a doctor," Max said. "Doctors help people."

"I help people."

"You help evil people do evil things."

"This is Syria. We do not have much choice in such matters."

Max sat him up again—only to punch him in the face and knock him down. "Tell me about BK-16."

Blood trickled out of the Surgeon's left nostril, but he said nothing.

Max kicked him in the gut, making him cry out in pain. "Tell me about BK-16."

The Surgeon laughed. "People are going to die."

Tom moved in, propped the Surgeon up, and said, "We could turn you over to FSA so they can get their men's organs back."

The Surgeon frowned. "I don't have their organs. I sold them."

"But you do have your own organs, don't you?" Max said. "Inside your body."

The Surgeon didn't reply.

Max smiled. "I can't promise that the removals will be as neat as your surgeries, but I'm sure the FSA will do their best with what they have."

The Surgeon stiffened up.

Max watched and waited.

The Surgeon cleared his throat, spitting up blood. "BK-16 is a man-made virus to be used for assassination. After the target is infected, he loses consciousness—I'm not exactly sure why. Soon he regains consciousness and seems normal, but in about five days, the virus dies and decomposes into kuznetsovine, a poison that kills the person. Because BK-16's deadly effect takes about five days, it's difficult to figure out who first introduced it to the target or how it was administered."

"Is there a cure for it?" Max asked.

"I don't know."

Max and Tom just glared at him.

"I really don't know," the Surgeon said. "Dr. Kuznetsov would know—he created it."

Tom looked over at Max, a surprised look on his face. "Where is this doctor?" he asked.

"Sorrento, Italy," the Surgeon said. "He lives with the Russian mafia there. Their godfather is a former KGB officer who might still be working for Russia."

Max considered the players and their roles in this. After the fall of the Soviet Union, numerous intelligence officers were suddenly without jobs, and many went to work for various mafia factions or created their own. He pressed the issue. "I thought the Syrian government was behind this, not the Russians."

"Russia controls Syria," the Surgeon said. "Russia says *jump*; we say *how high*?"

"Can you give us the names of the Russian mafia members?" Tom asked.

"Some of them, yes," the Surgeon said.

As the Surgeon gave the names, Max recorded them on his phone and sent them to Willy.

"What else can you tell us about BK-16, Dr. Kuznetsov, or this Russian mafia?" Tom asked.

"That's all I know," the Surgeon said.

Max raised his hand to strike him again. "That's not good enough."

"I swear, that's all I know," the Surgeon insisted.

Max and Tom glared at the Surgeon, but he seemed to be telling the truth. Max put the gag, hood, and earphones back on their prisoner. The gag wasn't necessary here, high in the sky, but Max didn't want to forget it later.

"We could be infected," Tom said.

"I'm not going to let you die," Max said. "I promised Dad that I'd take care of you."

"I can take care of myself," Tom said. "And you need to take care of yourself."

"Maybe we're not poisoned."

"Does Willy have the results of our blood and urine analyses yet?"

"Still waiting," Max said.

"He better hurry."

———— ◉ ————

THE CHINOOK SWIFTLY crossed into Turkey and flew five hundred klicks in less than an hour and a half to Incirlik Air Base, where it landed. Off to the side of the helo pad were parked two black SUVs. Inside one sat two buff dudes. From the other SUV stepped a man wearing blue jeans, long hair, and a bandana. He looked like Willy Nelson in his late forties. His real name was Willy Madison, and he was their boss and a family friend. Uncharacteristic for Willy, his neck and shoulders sagged as if he were carrying a heavy load.

Max humped his kit off the helo and watched Willy from the corner of his eye. "Something's wrong."

Willy approached them with open arms. "Bravo, bravo."

Max and Tom loaded their kit in the back of his truck before Willy gave each of them a fatherly hug, but his hug seemed tired. "What's wrong?" Tom asked.

Willy hesitated. When he spoke, his New Orleans twang lost its spring: "I'll tell you in the brief." He motioned for them to load up in the van.

Max road shotgun. *Sounds serious.*

Tom hopped in back. "What about the Surgeon?"

Willy started the engine. "My guys in the other vehicle will take care of him."

The two buff dudes left the other truck and boarded the helo, but Max was too concerned about the results of the blood and urine tests to give them a second thought.

Max feared for his brother but hoped for the best.

"Any luck with tracing the Russian who threatened to kill Max and me?" Tom asked.

"The caller spoofed a cell number in Damascus, but we're still working on trying to find the original source," Willy said.

Chapter Fifteen

Charcoal-like clouds formed in the morning sky as Max, Tom, and Willy rode past hornbeam and Lebanese cedar trees. After passing some office buildings, they went through a roundabout. Black pines stood as ominous sentinels. Willy turned onto a road with a soulless strip of bars and restaurants with English names like Aqua Bar and Red Onion Restaurant that catered to US servicemen. They rolled through a residential area for a few blocks before pulling up to an isolated gray house, its yard decayed and its windows facing out like vacant eyes.

Willy parked the SUV, and Max and Tom grabbed their bags and got out. Willy walked up to the door with them. Thick cobwebs hung from the eaves, and fungi spread over cracks in the wood.

Willy unlocked the front door, and they passed through an arched doorway. The floors were dark brown, as were the walls and ceiling, and the air tasted stale. Even with the curtains open and the lights on, the place was dark. It felt like walking into a tomb.

In the living room on a sofa sat a man who Max hadn't seen before and a woman he recognized. She was unpardonably pretty. Max had worked with her years ago in Syria, when he was a Navy SEAL in Team Six. Tom had been there, too, as an Army Ranger. In the winter of last year, she'd briefly helped Max and Tom again.

"Hannah!" Max said.

She stood, and her smile brightened the gloom. "Max! And Tom!"

Then she introduced the man Max hadn't seen before. "I'd like you to meet my teammate and good friend, Chris Paladin."

"Good meeting you," Chris said.

Max nodded politely, but he preferred talking to Hannah.

He was about to ask her a question when Tom blurted out like a machine gun, "Chris Paladin, it's an honor. You were a SEAL with

Team Six in western Iraq. I was with the 75th Rangers. We came later as part of the same task force to stop Syrians from smuggling terrorists and IEDs across the border into Iraq."

Max shot Tom an annoyed glance.

Chris didn't say anything.

Hannah worked for CIA on the same task force, recruiting spies. Max looked at her, but she was focused on Chris. Max suspected that he was more than simply a "teammate and good friend" to her, and he couldn't help feeling a bit jealous.

Chris looked at Max, who felt as if his private thoughts had been busted. Max cleared his throat and said to Hannah, "Have you heard from Sonny?"

"Sonny's leg recovered from that last op he did with you guys, and he was working with us over in Istanbul, but JSOC needed him for something." The Joint Special Operations Command was in charge of Tier One units such as SEAL Team Six and Sonny's unit, the Army's Delta Force.

"Did JSOC say why?" Max asked.

Hannah shook her head. "Do they ever? I'm hoping he can join us soon."

"Kickass," Max said.

Tom was still excited: "A CIA tech wizard named Young Park was captured by terrorists, and you guys rescued him. Your call sign was Reverend. You were a legend."

"*Is* a legend," Hannah said proudly.

Chris shrugged his shoulders, as if uncomfortable with the praise.

The wattage in Hannah's smile dimmed and her eyes met Max's, and she said, "I'm sorry about your dad. He was a real standup guy."

"He was," Tom said.

"The best," Max said.

Chris lowered his head. "I'm sorry for your loss."

There was a moment of silence.

Willy spoke up: "Hank wasn't the kind of man to let a good chair go to waste." He plopped his keister in a stuffed chair. "And he had no *troque* with the sentimental." Willy was partly right. Hank had no barter with the sentimental, but when it came to his wife, Hank was a sentimental idiot. After her death, he was never the same.

Max and Tom sat in separate love seats, and Chris and Hannah returned to their perch on the sofa.

Willy looked at Hannah as if to signal her to begin the brief.

"Chris, Sonny, and I discovered an assassin," she said. "He goes by the codename Falcon. We put him under surveillance to find out more about his next target and who he's working for. Three nights ago, we followed him to a soccer game. Unknown to us, CIA's Chief of Station in Turkey, Bill Hart, and some other VIPs were in attendance at the same game. When we spotted Bill and the others, I got word to him he might be the target of an assassination plot, and the assassin was in the stadium. Bill told me about a brush with a stranger who had scratched his arm with something. At the time of the incident, he thought it was an accident. I asked Bill to describe the stranger, and his description matched Falcon's appearance—right down to the clothes he was wearing that night. Although we had Falcon under surveillance, we hadn't watched him every second, and it was likely that he scratched Bill with an object dipped in some sort of poison." Hannah turned to Willy.

"The poison is called BK-16, but Max will get to that in minute," Willy said, then picked up where Hannah left off: "Bill passed out before he made it to his car. His security guys rushed him to the hospital, where he remained unconscious. The hospital staff couldn't figure out what was wrong with him, so he was flown to our regional military hospital in Landstuhl, Germany. After eight hours of unconsciousness, he came to, but we kept him in Landstuhl until we got the results of his blood and urine tests."

"The same night that Bill became ill, we rendered Falcon," Hannah said. "Our techs unlocked his smartphone and found multiple phone calls to Bulgaria, which our people are still investigating. Russia has used Bulgaria as a cutout for its dirty work before, so it's possible they were behind the plot to kill Bill. Falcon and his people are suspicious of the Russians, but if Falcon thought he was working for a radical Islamic organization, he could've easily become Russia's puppet. Also on his phone, our techs found web searches for information about Bill. Currently, Falcon is being interrogated at one of our black sites, but he hasn't given us anything significant yet."

Max knew that he and his brother might've been poisoned, but hearing Hannah's report seemed to confirm it. He felt as if the floor had been pulled out from underneath him—not so much at his own impending death but more at the death of his brother.

"Thanks, Hannah," Willy said. "That same evening, in Damascus, Max and Tom ate at a local restaurant, and soon after, Max lost most of his consciousness and Tom passed out cold. We analyzed the blood and urine samples for Bill, Max, and Tom, but were unable to discover signs of poisoning, drugs, or any known virus."

Willy turned to Max, who took his turn. "We captured a man who calls himself the Surgeon. He'd been experimenting with BK-16 on anti-Assad militants and recently expanded his victim pool to others. The Surgeon told us that BK-16 is a virus engineered specifically for assassination. Like Hannah reported, after the target is infected, he loses consciousness, but then he seems normal again. Approximately five days after the infection, the virus dies in the bloodstream and decomposes into a poison called kuznetsovine, which is what kills the target."

"Are all three of their poisonings related?" Chris asked.

"Because of the Bulgaria connection, Langley suspects that the Russians are behind the plot to kill Bill Hart," Willy said. "The poisoning of Max and Tom seems to be Syrian—someone didn't like them snooping around in their neighborhood or wanted to get rid of them for whatever other reason. We're still working on it, but this is our best theory so far."

"Is there a cure?" Hannah asked.

"The Surgeon didn't know," Max said.

Tom chimed in. "The Surgeon told us that a Dr. Kuznetsov would know if there's a cure—he created BK-16. He lives in a house in Italy run by Russian mafia."

Willy took the floor: "When Max and Tom sent in that piece of intel, we ran it down. The leader of that gang of Russian mobsters is Nestor Orlav. He works for FSB and owns some legitimate business in construction and waste management, but he and his men have been suspected of murder, kidnapping, torture, extortion, drug trafficking, hijacking, and other crimes. We believe that Orlav and his men have intimidated and bribed witnesses and the courts to avoid prosecution. One of his men was arrested for killing his pregnant wife, which made the news, but now he's only serving time on a reduced sentence for loan sharking."

Willy looked around the room, stood up with an iPhone in his hand, looked down at it for a moment and tapped on it. Then he looked at everyone again. "Your mission is to capture Dr. Kuznetsov alive. He's our link to find a cure for Bill, Max, and Tom. And to prevent future assassinations. I've sent an encrypted file to each of your phones with photos of Orlav and his crew. If they threaten you or the mission, kill them. There may be innocent civilians in that house, so be careful not to harm them, unless they become a threat."

"All four of us on this mission?" Max asked.

Willy snarled like a wolf protecting his territory. "The more the merrier. The four of you will fly directly from Turkey to Naval Support Activity, Naples, Italy. Time ain't exactly on our side."

Max stood. "Let's do it."

Tom rose to his feet, too. "Yeah."

Chris and Hannah got on their feet, too.

Max and the others loaded their kit into the SUV. Max and Tom finished first, and Willy called them to his room. There they waited to see what he wanted.

Willy handed out his hand to Tom. "Your pistol."

Tom seemed confused. "Huh?"

Max didn't understand either.

Willy gave them both looks like they were stupid, and he spoke louder: "The CZ 75 that Gus lent you."

"Oh, yeah." Tom handed over the pistol, ammo, hip holster, and pouches he'd received at the US Interests Section in the Czech Embassy in Damascus.

"And the phone," Willy said.

Tom gave him that, too.

Willy set them aside and pulled out a Glock from a diplomatic bag. He handed it to Tom along with ammo, holster, ammo pouches, and a phone, which were also in the pouch. "Don't lose these."

"I won't."

Willy put the Czech weapon and kit in the dip bag, closed it, and locked it.

"Hear anything on Dad's killer?" Max asked.

"Still working on it," Willy said. "That's the main reason I wanted a minute with you two alone. Have either of you heard the phrase 'Cruel Odysseus'?"

It sounded familiar—Max thought hard. "In Berlin."

"Yeah," Tom said. "Heard it or read it there."

"Why?" Max asked.

"Before your dad was killed," Willy said, "that phrase kept popping up in intel reports. Now it's popping up again."

"In what context has it been popping up?" Max asked.

"The context of just before someone important is killed," Willy said.

"Can you tell us more?" Tom asked.

Willy put a hand on each of their shoulders. "I don't have anything more, but when I do, you two will be the first to know." He led Max and Tom out of the house, and they piled into the van with Chris and Hannah.

"What was that about?" Hannah asked.

"I needed to account for some lost equipment and give them replacements," Willy said nonchalantly.

She seemed satisfied with his answer, or at least, she didn't pry further.

More black clouds gathered, and the sky grew darker. Willy made a phone call, something about a helo pickup, and he started up the engine. He was still on the phone as he pulled away from the gray house and continued down the street.

Max turned to Chris and said, "Heard you went off to a monastery or something."

"Went to college and became a pastor," Chris said.

Max scratched his head. "You're here now; does that mean you quit being a preacher?"

"I'm a pastor full time. And I do contract work for the Agency part time."

Max wasn't moved by Chris's words.

Tom leaned forward. "I'm a student full time, and I do this part time, too."

"Good," Chris said. "Which school?"

"Georgetown," Tom said.

Chris raised his eyebrows. "Outstanding."

"Where'd you study to be a pastor?" Tom asked.

"Harvard."

"Harvard—wow—Harvard. Didn't know they had a college for being a pastor."

Chris smiled. "Harvard has been training ministers since its beginning. The divinity school was established in the early 1800s."

Max wasn't feeling the love. "You were great in the day, but how do we know you haven't lost your fighting edge? Being a preacher and all, how do we know you won't hesitate to pull the trigger?"

Chris didn't seem fazed. "Being a preacher hasn't stopped me from killing or capturing bad men. As for fighting edge, I guess Langley thinks I'm good enough."

"If good enough gets my brother or me killed, then good enough ain't good enough."

"When the bullets start flying, you can be the judge of whether I still have what it takes."

"By then it's too late," Max said. "And don't count on God to drop down from the sky and save us from evil."

"Give it a rest, Max," Tom said.

Chris remained unperturbed. "I understand. You have an issue with God, not me. I don't take it personally. Good things really do happen, Max."

Max shifted uncomfortably in his seat. "Not in my world. Why are you really here?"

Chris looked him in the eye. "Because the Lord has work for us to do."

Chapter Sixteen

Willy led Max, Tom, Chris, and Hannah onto a ghost-white Lockheed L-100, the civilian version of the military's C-130. On it was painted the logo for a cover company, L3 Technologies, masking the espionage and paramilitary nature of their mission. They took their seats and buckled up, and soon the plane lifted off. Over the speakers, Willy played "Highwayman," performed by outlaw country musicians Johnny Cash, Waylon Jennings, Willie Nelson, and Kris Kristofferson. Although Max was more into classic rock than country, every time Willy played "Highwayman," it felt like the beginning of something epic.

When the song finished, Willy spoke in a loud voice so everyone could hear him clearly over the sound of the plane's engines. "Hannah will be in charge of this mission, and she'll answer to me. Any objections?" It didn't seem like a real question because he didn't wait for a real answer. "I didn't think so." Willy disappeared into the galley, and soon the scent of food floated into the cabin.

Half an hour later, Willy returned with grub: hot blueberry pancakes, bacon, and eggs. Max, Chris, and Willy wolfed them down. Hannah ate like a civilized person, and Tom nibbled like a rabbit. They drank coffee, except for Chris, who had orange juice. The world slowed down, and everyone seemed to be dozing off except Willy.

Max woke to the smell of lunch and a dark cabin. For a moment, he thought he was dreaming. He pressed the light on his watch: he'd fallen asleep for five hours. The cabin lights came on, and Tom and the others woke, too.

"Aren't you going to tell Tom?" Willy asked.

Max rubbed the sleepy out of his eyes. "Tell him what?"

"About school," Willy said.

"What?" Tom asked.

Max didn't say anything.

Willy gave him a look that said, *Tell him.*

Max gave in. "I'm graduating from college."

Willy left and disappeared into the galley.

"I knew you were taking some classes," Tom said, "but I didn't know you were graduating. Why all the secrecy?"

"I didn't think it was important," Max said. "Willy told me to finish my degree, or CIA would boot me out. I don't know if it was true or not, but I did it."

"Which college?"

"University of Maryland University College."

"That's a great school," Tom said.

"People say 'it's a great school' when they mean 'it's not a great school.'"

"I really mean it."

"It's not like your Georgetown." Then Max pointed his nose at Chris. "Or Mr. Harvard over there."

"You could've gone to either of those schools," Tom said. "Why didn't you?"

"I'd already done some distance learning with UMUC when I was in the Navy, and it's one of the top online colleges for vets—so I could continue working at CIA while attending college. It just made sense."

"You've always been smarter than me, but you like to hide it."

"I've always had to work at learning," Max said. "You were always the smart one."

"Growing up, Dad wasn't around much, and you had to raise me and stay on top of your schoolwork, too. You're the hardest worker I know. When's the graduation ceremony?"

"Don't know."

"How can you not know?"

"Not going."

"Why not?" Tom asked.

"I got my diploma to keep working for the government, not for some dog-and-pony show."

"Congratulations, you're graduating before me."

Max smiled.

After half an hour, everyone except Tom had finished eating, and the plane made its descent. Off the port side appeared Mount Vesuvius—the infamous volcano that unleashed a hundred thousand times the thermal energy of a nuclear bomb and destroyed Pompeii and other cities of the Roman Empire. Now the volcano was a lush green, its cities resurrected from the ashes and lava rock.

The Gulf of Naples glistened in the sunlight. Their plane landed hard and spunky and came to a screeching halt on the runway of US Naval Support Activity Naples, forcing Max hard against his seatbelt. It reminded him of military landings when the pilots were all about getting it done *tout de suite*. It was hell for the plane, but Max liked it.

The Italian military owned the base, but the US managed its day-to-day activities. A similar arrangement had been at the center of the Sigonella Crisis in 1985. Four Palestinian terrorists had hijacked the cruise ship MS *Achille Lauro* and killed Jewish American Leon Klinghoffer. The terrorists escaped to Egypt, where their mastermind, Abu Abbas, joined them, and they attempted to escape by airliner. American F-14 fighter jets forced the terrorists to land at Naval Air Station Sigonella in Italy. Max knew of the eighty SEAL Team Six and Delta Force operators who surrounded the terrorists' plane, but three hundred Italian military police surrounded the operators. Italian Prime Minister Bettino Craxi got his way, and the terrorists were turned over to his government, which released mastermind Abbas but convicted the four terrorists. Six years later, two of the terrorists were released on parole. Max fully understood that the Italian government could take charge of this base at any time, and that Italy had a history of being soft on terrorists.

Max's plane taxied to a halt where a van was parked near the runway. Beside the van stood a man who looked like a young Bradley Cooper wearing sunglasses.

A ground crew promptly positioned air stairs in front of the plane's hatch. Willy opened the hatch and said, "The guy with the van, his name is Angelo Figus. He's an asset of ours who will take you to the yacht—your safe house for this mission."

Max, Tom, Chris, and Hannah grabbed their bags and descended the air stairs.

The van was a gray Fiat Ducato, its engine running. "I'm Angelo. Welcome to Naples."

"Grazie," Tom and Hannah said.

"Thank you," Chris said.

Max didn't frown. Nor did he smile. He just said, "Thanks." Italy's behavior after the *Achille Lauro* hijacking didn't endear the country to Max, and although he liked Bradley Cooper's performance in *The Hangover* and *American Sniper*, he didn't like Cooper's Hollywood liberalism. Angelo's nationality and appearance were already two strikes against him; one more strike and Angelo was out.

They loaded into the van. Angelo took the wheel, and they spun away. The Italian gate guards checked the IDs of military personnel entering the base, but they didn't check the IDs of people leaving. Max's team rolled through the gates and entered town, where they passed a sign that read: MMP Ristorante & Pizzeria.

He quickly forgot about the *Achille Lauro* and Cooper. "I want to eat some pizza."

"You just ate," Tom reminded him.

"Pizza sounds good," Chris said.

Angelo accelerated. "Naples is the birthplace of pizza—would you like me to stop?"

Maybe Angelo isn't so bad, Max thought.

"Maybe later," Hannah said sweetly.

"We'll need some Neapolitan ice cream, too," Max said.

"That's from Naples, too," Angelo said. "We call it *spumoni*."

Hannah kept her cool. "Later."

"I'm already looking forward to our next meal," Chris said.

"Angelo, are you from Naples?" Tom asked.

Angelo turned onto a highway. "No. I'm from Sardinia. But I go where the Agency sends me." He followed the highway northeast before it curved around south.

"When we arrive at the marina in Naples, we'll split up," Hannah said. "Two of us will drive the van to the front of Doctor Kuznetsov's place and take a video of it. The other two will go by yacht and film the back of the place."

Max spoke up first: "Tom and I can take the yacht."

"Works for me," Chris said.

"We should go in different pairings," Hannah said. "Max and I in one pair and Chris and Tom in the other."

"Tom and I are used to working together," Max said. "Same as you and Chris."

"I understand," Hannah said. "But when it comes to your brother, I'm concerned that you might prioritize his safety over the mission. And when it comes to Chris, I don't want him to prioritize my safety over the mission. I simply want us to put the mission before our personal relations."

"Okay," Tom said.

Max wasn't feeling the same. Even so, Hannah was captivating, and he didn't mind spending more time with her. "Let's do it," he said.

Chris looked as if he'd gulped down a drink of toxic waste, but he didn't verbalize it.

Angelo drove to the coast and followed it southeast toward Sorrento on the spur of the bay. Mount Vesuvius towered above them at over twelve hundred meters high. The highway branched off and ran beside a canal that guided them to a marina, where there were numerous berths for boats, yachts, and super yachts. The marina opened out to the Port of Naples, shaped like a giant sparkling amphitheater with boats sailing across its stage.

Angelo parked the van and left the keys in the ignition for Chris and Tom, who assumed command of the vehicle. Max, Hannah, and Angelo got out and carried their bags across the pier. Angelo had a shit-eating grin on his face, both arms swinging freely, seeming comfortable walking with his new posse. Max strolled beside him carrying his bags. Max's sunglasses hid his eyes from outsiders while he scanned for threats, in addition to protecting them from the sun. Hannah smiled serenely, and her bulky bag didn't slow her down a step.

The trio boarded a Pershing 62, a cross between a muscle-boat and a motoryacht. "I had the engines customized to run quiet," Angelo said cheerfully.

"Studly," Max said. He rushed below and stowed his kit in a twin cabin. Hannah stashed hers in a separate cabin. The engine rumbled. It was quieter than any yacht he'd ever heard.

Max climbed up the stairs and hurried out onto the pier, where he untied the lines from the cleats on the dock. Hannah helped. Then they secured the lines and boat fenders, and the yacht pulled away from the dock.

Angelo skillfully maneuvered their vessel through a maze of boats and piers in the marina. When they reached the open bay, they passed between a ship and two yachts, the only other vessels nearby. The salt in the air tasted familiar to Max, and the breeze felt good. He was at home with Mother Ocean. Hannah and Angelo seemed comfortable, too.

"Where'd you learn how to pilot a boat so well?" Max asked.

Angelo smiled. "My father is a fisherman."

Max shifted from casual curiosity to a more pointed question. "Does he like America?"

"He doesn't say one way or the other."

"But you do."

Angelo pointed his body and feet forward. "I like America, don't get me wrong, but I don't do this job for America—I do this for Italy. I hate what the socialists are doing to my country."

"You get paid for this, don't you?"

"A man has to do something for a living. And I get to serve my country, too. In Italy, we say, *Prendere due piccioni con una fava.* It means, 'catch two pigeons with one fava bean.' Similar to your 'kill two birds with one stone.'"

"Ah, you feed the birds instead of eating them," Max said.

Angelo shrugged his shoulders. "You get paid for this, don't you?"

Max smiled. "I do. A man's got to do something for a living. Prendere due piccioni con una fava."

Angelo grinned. As he motored south, Max and Hannah examined the photos on their phones of Dr. Kuznetsov, FSB godfather Nestor Orlav, and the other mafia members.

They sailed ten klicks south to tree-topped cliffs that rose high above the ocean. Angelo cut off the engine and dropped anchor. He pointed to shore. "There, that little house near sea level in the gap between the cliffs—that's the back of it, where Doctor Kuznetsov lives."

Max went aft and sat on the white leather cushioned benches on the sun deck. Hannah joined him. Max pulled out a video camera from his bag, powered it up, and took a look at maximum telephoto range. On the back of the house was a pair of solid wooden doors. The patio extended out onto the beach, where three men stood talking. They had bulging muscles, tattoos, and hard faces. They weren't armed with rifles, but it seemed likely they'd carry concealed pistols. Nine beach chairs sat empty around them.

A tiled corridor bordered with potted plants lined the right side of the house, where a fourth man appeared. Max recognized him from the photos that Willy sent—a brigadier, Yuri Romashkov, who reported to the godfather. He walked across the patio before going inside. A fifth man roved back and forth on the beach as if on patrol. The three men on the patio continued to chat.

"How many enemies total, you think?" Hannah asked.

"Fifteen or twenty."

"We haven't seen the doctor," Hannah said.

"Or Godfather Orlav," Max said. He looked at the photos on his iPhone again.

Max and Hannah watched and waited for fifteen minutes, but nothing seemed to change. Max's thoughts drifted to Hannah. He wondered if her pairing with him on the yacht was a convenient excuse so she could be alone with him. Hoping his hunch was true, he asked her, "What is it you see in Chris?"

Hannah seemed to ponder the question. "Could you get me something to drink?" she asked. "I'll watch the target area."

"Sure." Max went below and opened the refrigerator. Inside were plastic bottles of water. He took out two, went above deck, and handed one to Hannah. Max didn't know if she was truly thirsty or if she was giving herself time to think. "Well?" he asked patiently.

Hannah screwed off the cap and took a sip of water. "Chris is my most loyal friend and one of the best operators in the business."

"You look at him like he's more than a friend, and he looks at you that way, too."

"I admire him, but our relationship is professional—there's no way it could be personal."

"Why not?" Max took a drink, and the liquid cooled the back of his throat.

"I'm not interested in men," Hannah said matter-of-factly.

"I don't understand."

"Birds of a feather flock together."

Max tried to breathe and swallow his drink at the same time, and he sputtered. He wiped the water off his mouth. His shirt was wet, but it would dry soon. *What a waste*, he thought. "Have you ever kissed a guy?"

"Never."

Max took another drink. This time, he didn't choke on it. "Aren't you curious what it'd be like?"

"Are you curious what it'd be like to kiss a guy?" she asked kindly.

Max wanted to spit out his water again, but he held it in without choking on it. "Not curious. Not at all."

"It's like that," she said. "I'm not interested. Not at all."

After his intimate exchange with Hannah, he went mute. Max returned his eyes to the camera monitor and tried to focus on it, as if everything was okay. But he was still in shock at Hannah's revelation. As he tried to focus on his work, a man resembling the doctor stepped out onto the patio.

"That's him in the T-shirt and shorts," Max said. "Isn't it?"

Hannah studied the monitor intently. "Sure does look like him."

After a brief conversation with one of the hard-faced men, the doctor returned inside. Max and Hannah watched for several more minutes, but he didn't reappear.

"I think we have enough video," Max said.

Hannah's words flowed like honey: "Angelo, can you take us back to the marina?"

CIA officers were habitual liars, and it occurred to Max that Hannah was using the lesbian story as an excuse to avoid becoming personally involved with him, but he didn't know her well, and for now he assumed it to be true. *What a waste*, he couldn't help thinking again.

Angelo fired up the engine and pushed the throttle ahead one-third. The water behind churned. He steered to the north, and the yacht picked up speed, rumbling beneath Max's feet. After they put more distance between themselves and Doctor Kuznetsov's house, Angelo pushed the throttle to two-thirds, and then full speed ahead. A rooster tail of water rose behind them.

"We should try to snatch this doc tonight," Max said.

Chapter Seventeen

Max couldn't wait for the hunt to begin. Or for dinner. Angelo had sailed the yacht back to the marina in Naples, but they had to wait for Chris and Tom to return. At last they sauntered down the dock, and he hungrily eyed the pizza Tom carried aboard while Chris went below to put the spumoni in the freezer. Finally Chris joined everyone on a couch that wrapped around a table on the main deck. They dug into the pizza like a pack of wolves—even Tom. The pizza crust tasted softer and chewier, the tomato fresher, and the basil stronger than the American pizza Max was used to.

Angelo activated a pop-up monitor on a cabinet and played Max and Hannah's surveillance video. Because Max had already seen it and nothing much happened, it was like watching paint dry, so he focused more on his pizza.

Angelo turned to him and said, "This is called Pizza Margherita, cooked on a wood-burning stove. The tomatoes are grown in the volcanic soil of Mount Vesuvius. And the mozzarella comes from the milk of water buffalos."

Max grunted his approval.

"It's really good," Chris said.

Hannah swallowed a bite. "I love Italian pizza."

Tom nodded politely. He wasn't as enthusiastic as the others about the food.

A fly hovered over Max's plate. Angelo had a newspaper on his pilot chair, so Max reached over, grabbed the paper, and with one swing, he batted the insect out of the air. The fly landed on the deck motionless.

Max was pleased with himself and his masterful kill. "It was a quick death."

The fly buzzed: *Bzz.* Silence. *Bzz. Bzz.* Then the fly crawled around on the deck. *Bzz-bzz, bzz-bzz.* Max hit it—hard—and once again for good measure. It lay there squashed, and there was no more buzzing.

Tom chuckled. "Not so quick."

Max gave him the stink eye.

They finished the first video and then watched Chris and Tom's, but it was simply two cars parked in front of the curb and two parked in the driveway. "If four people came in each car," Chris said, "We're dealing with sixteen people."

"Unless some came by taxi," Max said.

"Or less came in each car," Hannah said.

After Chris and Tom's video ended, Angelo displayed a Google map on the monitor. There was an area behind the front wall of the house with five lawn chairs and some potted plants.

Tom finished his last bite of pizza. "Doesn't appear to be any video surveillance at the house."

Chris went below and retrieved the carton of spumoni and some spoons and bowls. He scooped the spumoni into the bowls and served them. Unlike American pink, white, and brown Neapolitan ice cream, this was green, white, and red, like the Italian flag.

Hannah was looking down at her phone and hadn't started to eat dessert yet. "I just received a text that Sonny might join us tomorrow or the following day."

"Boo-yah," Max said.

"That's great," Chris said.

"We could use the help," Tom added.

Max ate a spoonful of each color of his spumoni. The green part was pistachio, white was vanilla, and the red was cherry. Whip cream was mixed in, and between the layers were pistachio nuts and bits of cherry. "I was telling Hannah that I'd like to wrap up the doctor tonight," he said.

"That place might be different at night," Chris said. "A night surveillance might give us more intel."

Tom often played devil's advocate, but he quietly ate the green pistachio section of his spumoni.

Angelo mixed a spoonful of red and white and ate without a word.

Max put his spoon down. "It'd be great to do a night of surveillance before we go in. And wait 'til Sonny arrives. But that target could harden while we wait. Or the doctor could disappear. Or Tom and I could die from this virus. Or any slew of other things could happen. I'd rather snatch the doctor sooner than later."

"Tonight's fine with me," Chris said. "If we go in quiet, we'll have a better chance of surviving—maybe FN P90s." The FN P90 was smaller than an assault rifle yet bigger than a pistol—a submachine gun.

"P90s sound good," Max said. He carried the Belgian sound-suppressed weapon in his gear. They were purchased through a European cutout, and their serial numbers were filed off—making them difficult to trace to the US.

"My call sign is still Reverend," Chris said, "and Hannah is still Infidel."

"I'm Yukon," Max said, "and Tom is Tomahawk."

Angelo smiled. "Bradley."

"Same plan as this morning?" Hannah asked. "Chris and Tom enter from the street, and Max and I hit from the beach."

Chris ran a hand through his hair and rubbed the back of his neck—he appeared agitated.

Max didn't like the pairings either. "Like I mentioned earlier, I think Tom and I work better together, and you and Chris know each other's moves better. This morning was clear skies and sunshine, but tonight there's a strong chance of thunder and lightning. Surveillance is one thing, but assault is another."

"I'm with Max on this one," Chris said. "Hannah and I can assault from the water, and Max and Tom assault from the street."

"Works for me," Max said. He looked to his brother for support.

"Sure," Tom said.

Angelo remained immersed in his spumoni and avoided the discussion.

Hannah ate a bite of spumoni and swallowed. Then she drank from her bottled water. The expression on her face was neutral. "Okay."

"I'd like to keep the van here at the marina," Chris said. "If Hannah or I get injured, we'll need a vehicle to get to the base hospital."

"Can we get a different car for the assault?" Max asked.

Angelo had eaten the last of his spumoni and set down his spoon. "I can get another car for tonight. Should I go now?"

"Yes, that'd be great," Tom said.

Angelo nodded before hustling off, and Max and the others spent the next two hours planning: weather, visibility, surf conditions, communication, and so on.

The sky darkened, and when Angelo returned with an extra car, Chris and Hannah discussed the yacht insertion and extraction with him. Then everyone kitted up.

Max wore civilian clothes—a dark brown shirt and light gray trousers. His clothing, weapons, and kit were sterile, nothing with tags or serial numbers that could be connected to the US. He concealed a compact Glock 19 pistol in an abdomen holster inside his waistband, which he covered with his untucked shirt. In a cargo pocket he carried an Italian inflatable life vest. If he was escaping and evading, he could ditch other items to lighten his load and hasten his flight, but these items he'd keep on him until the death.

He dropped an ear bud the size of a pencil eraser into his ear canal, a magnetized receiver that he could fish out after the mission with a paperclip. Max attached his throat mic and strapped on his FN P90 submachine gun loaded with fifty rounds of ammo. He carried two extra magazines on the support side of his shoulder harness. In a small backpack, he placed flex cuffs, a black hood, gag, and noise-cancelling earphones—all to control the prisoner—and a pair of night vision goggles (NVGs).

For protection, bullet-resistant vests weren't perfect, and even the best ones weakened after taking several hits. Max didn't like one slowing him down, and this time was no different—he counted on speed, surprise, and violence of action to keep him and his teammates alive.

Chapter Eighteen

Max became nervous—terribly nervous. He'd done this sort of op more times than he could remember, and he'd never had such jitters, so he didn't understand why this was happening now. If he let it get the best of him, it'd be a problem, but he wielded it as a weapon. The anxiety intensified his focus and raised his energy level, and come heaven or hell, he'd see this to the end.

Knowing that his brother was infected with a deadly virus bothered him. Acquaintances and friends came and went, but family was always there, and Tom was the only family Max had left. His adrenaline spread like wildfire through his veins. Max would kill the FSB godfather, his brigadier, and any other two-bit-piss-drinking-knuckle-dragging-no-nuts-Russian-mafia-monkey who stood between him and snatching Dr. Kuznetsov.

Max carried a human-sized duffel bag with a tranquilizer hypodermic in the side pocket—a present for Dr. Kuznetsov. He stored the bag in the back seat of the black Fiat Tipo sedan Angelo had acquired for them before he sat in the passenger seat next to Tom.

Tom fired up the engine and drove from the marina. Through the black of night, he steered out onto Strada Statale 145. "You know, having a reverend around might be good luck," Tom said.

Max shook his head in disbelief. "You sound like *maman*." He used the French word for their mother. Tom wasn't old enough to remember her when she was alive, but Max was. "She believed in God and priests, and none of that saved her."

Ahead, a bonfire blazed beside the road. A city sanitation truck dumped trash into the flames.

"What the hell?" Max asked. "The city's going to burn their trash right there? Beside the road?"

"The mafia controls a lot of the municipal waste disposal," Tom said. "They sneak around at night and dump metals, chemicals, and household and industrial waste on whatever land they find. Then they burn it."

"That can't be good for the people who live near the burning trash."

"The Italians are discovering an increase of cancer in children. Probably adults, too."

"Can't the government kick out the mafia?" Max asked.

"The government is in bed with the mafia."

They passed the toxic fire. The street carried them south under overpasses, between barricades, and out of the city, where small plots of farmland emerged. Cars on the road became scarce, and the shadowy arms and fingers of trees grasped at their headlights. A black mountain loomed, pushing at their vehicle as if to shove them off the road and into the black Bay of Naples. Lights from a handful of resort hotels guided them south, away from the phantom mountain. Up on a tuff cliff perched the coastal town of Vico Equense. Their street climbed out of the city before it squeezed into hairpin turns over a small mountain.

Max and his brother arrived in Sorrento, the city where their target was located. Chris broke squelch once on his radio, indicating that he and Hannah were in place behind the target building. As planned, Chris and Hannah would have to wait. Max donned his night vision goggles and switched them on.

Tom parked to the side of Dr. Kuznetsov's house. Max broke squelch on the radio once, signaling that they were in place, too.

Chris broke squelch twice: *ready to assault.*

This was the point of no return. Max could call it off, and the doc and the Russian mafia wouldn't be wiser. If Max broke squelch twice, there was no putting the Easy Cheese spray back in the can.

Max broke squelch twice: *go.* He and Tom exited the car.

With Max as point man, they hustled along the walkway between two parked cars and a wall shielding the front of the house. The Russians had no idea what was about to befall them. A door squeaked open somewhere, but Max wasn't sure exactly where the sound came from. Rather than hesitate, he turned the corner.

Two additional cars were in the driveway. As more of the driveway came in view, so did one of the Russian thugs, less than three meters away. He hadn't appeared in their surveillance videos, but he did appear in the photos that Willy had sent—his helmet-like hairstyle was unique from the others, who wore their hair short or shaved their heads bald. Helmet must've spotted Max because he reached to his waist for the pistol on his hip. Max lazed his forehead with his infrared beam and squeezed the trigger. The P90 emitted a click and a puff of air, and the Russian fell stiffly like a chopped tree.

The cliff to Max's left and a protruding section of the house to the right blocked most of Max's view to the beach in back of the property, but he could see along a sliver of an angle, past a line of potted plants to a boulder on the beach. More than fifty meters away, in front of the boulder, a roving patrol walked with a shotgun slung over his shoulder. He was only a second or less away from reaching Chris and Hannah's position. Max had to supercharge. He fired two shots in less than a second, hitting him both times in the upper body. Rover stopped. With the small caliber of his submachine gun, Max worried that Rover might keep going, so he shot him four more times. He dropped, and Max was pleased that he'd made the shots in time to save his friends.

He paused for a moment to see if more men appeared. When they didn't, he peeled right and entered a passageway between the wall and house, which was only wide enough for one person to pass through. He caught someone from behind. That someone must've heard Max because he spun around sporting a pistol in his hand. Max dispatched him with two to the head.

Max stepped over the body and examined the other side of the house, where the five lawn chairs were, and one man stood there smoking a cigarette. Max shook his head *no*, but the man went for his gun anyway. Max and Tom drilled him, and he fertilized the lawn.

Bang, bang! Two pistol shots were fired—by the Russians. It sounded as if the shots had come from the rear of the house.

"Man down," Chris's voice whispered.

Max's heart and stomach dropped together. *Hannah. Damn!*

"We need to medevac Infidel," Chris said.

"Leave Infidel there, grab the HVT, and we'll take Infidel out with us," Max said.

"I'm taking her out now."

"Don't abandon us," Max said. "We need to get the HVT."

"Bradley, Reverend," Chris said. "Need immediate extract."

"Okay," Angelo said.

Damn it!

Max reached the door in the middle of the house. He was pissed at Chris for abandoning him and his brother.

Tom tapped Max on the shoulder: *go.*

Max turned the doorknob. It was unlocked—*hallelujah*! He opened the door and slipped inside. The hall was clear. To the left was a door to a small area that might have been storage or a bathroom. Before he made noise clearing it, he wanted to take down the bigger rooms first, where there would likely be more people and more resistance—better to use surprise on the big fish than to waste it on the minnows. He came upon a closed door. Slowly and carefully he turned the knob. It was unlocked, too.

Max threw open the door.

A man wearing a goatee opened fire on him, slicing Max's shoulder. Max answered him with a flurry of shots that cast Goatee aside. Max expected a living room, but the furnishings seemed odd—three beds, a couch, and a TV. At the opposite end of the room, near the front door of the house, were two gargantuan guys, one bald and one with a buzz cut. Max ignored his wounded shoulder and kept moving. He peeled out of Tom's way, so his brother could pitch in. Baldy and Buzz got off shots, and one popped the air near Max's ear, but Max got off shots, too: two to the chest and one to the Baldy. Tom got a piece of Buzz and didn't stop popping him until Buzz was out of action.

There was a door to the left. Max turned the knob, but it was locked. He kicked hard near the doorknob, and the door flew open and the frame splintered. *Bang!* At first Max thought he'd been shot again, but then he saw the Brigadier, Yuri Romashkov, stagger back into a bathroom. He must've been standing directly behind the door, and the door hit him in the face with a bang. The Brigadier grabbed his nose with one hand and gripped a pistol with the other. He fell backwards over the toilet and knocked off a roll of toilet tissue, but he held on to his pistol.

Tom fired multiple times. The first shots hit the Brigadier in the shoulder. The last one capped his melon and spurt melon juice. A dripping sound echoed, but Max couldn't see if it came from the sink or the bathtub. He looked in the tub to see if anyone was there, but it was empty.

Max and Tom reversed roles, and Tom led them back around to the small room in the hall that they'd skipped over. The door must've been locked because Tom kicked it open and aimed inside. It was a small bathroom, where a man sat on a toilet with the seat down. Max couldn't figure out why Tom wasn't shooting, and then he realized that the man in front of them was Dr. Kuznetsov. *Jackpot!*

Max snatched him off his throne, bound his hands, gagged him, and put a black hood over his head while Tom covered the hall. Max yanked Doctor Kuznetsov out of the bathroom, shoved him through the hall, and out the door.

Max checked for threats left and right as he manhandled the doctor outside the house. He pushed the doctor past the cars and to their getaway car, the black Fiat. Max forced him onto the floorboard in back, where he sat with his feet on the doctor.

Now Tom was in the driver's seat, and he accelerated out of the immediate danger zone.

Ahead, police sirens shrieked and lights flashed. The sirens became louder and the lights brighter. Tom slowed down.

Uh-oh. It'd be difficult to explain the prisoner on the floorboard. But the police cars whizzed past them.

Max and Tom had captured the HVT. Proper planning and stealth were a deadly combination.

But they still had to find a cure for the virus. And Max hoped Hannah was okay.

Chapter Nineteen

The powerful muscle yacht sped through the darkness. Chris walked backwards, so he wouldn't trip on his swim fins, to the stern. Hannah did the same. They were two hundred meters from their target.

Chris turned and faced the black rooster tail of water spewing aft and grasped his face mask with one hand so it wouldn't get ripped off from the impact of hitting the water at high speed. He took a deep breath and jumped. He balled up so no appendages would stick out and break off, and somersaulted into the black abyss. Bubbly hands of water cradled his descent until violent hands twisted and turned him. Heaven became hell and hell became heaven, and right was left and left was right, and extra hands tossed him until he didn't know which way to go for oxygen.

Patience. He waited until the hands ceased tossing him. The buoyancy in his wetsuit raised him to the surface. He formed a tight circle with his lips and shot a bite of air to his lungs.

Where am I? The yacht's diesel engines hummed behind him, becoming fainter and fainter. From earlier planning, he knew it was headed south, the direction he needed to swim. He faced the noise, then kicked, stroked, and glided. To keep his profile to a minimum and remain quiet, he swam a modified sidestroke: a hybrid between sidestroke, breaststroke, and crawl.

Where's Hannah? Light from Doctor Kuznetsov's house glimmered on the water, but the base of a massive cliff blocked Chris's view of the actual house.

He noticed a bump in the water. Then he spotted the bump's shoulders. *Hannah.* He was relieved to find her. He caught up to her for a silent rendezvous, and they swam to shore together.

When the waters became shallow, they sat on large rocks and sand with water up to their shoulders and removed their fins, which they attached to bungee cords strapped over their backs. Hannah gave him a nod—*ready*.

Chris took the lead and slithered like a water snake to shore. He rose to a crouch and stalked onto dry land, where he removed his night vision goggles from a waterproof bag. After he switched on the goggles, the night turned green. The doctor's house cast a steady jade light on the waters, and a small bonfire created a flickering bloom of greenish white. He hugged the jagged volcanic wall of rock and edged closer. At the curve of a half circle formed by the bottom of the cliff, Chris stopped. The cliff blocked his view of the nearby boulder he'd seen during their surveillance, but he could see the other boulder, which marked the side of the house farthest from him.

He knew that Max and Tom had the more time-consuming route of traveling over land, and they needed more time to get into position, so Chris stood by to kill time. The only sound was his beating heart and the whispering ebb and flow of the tide.

After several minutes, Chris broke squelch on his radio. He received a single click in his ear bud—Max and Tom were in position, too.

Chris broke squelch twice—*standing by*. They'd reached the critical point. Max broke squelch twice. Now the genie couldn't be put back in the bottle. *Game on.*

He advanced toward the house. In his peripheral vision it looked like a man went down—possibly someone Max and Tom had taken out. Then, like a black wraith, a man with a pistol materialized from the darkness. Chris's whole body jerked with surprise. He aligned his laser on the specter's chest. The wraith aimed his pistol at him. Chris fired first—three to the chest and two to the head. *Tick-tick-tick. Tick-tick.* The wraith melted into the dirt.

Chris had become so occupied with the wraith that he hardly noticed a second man, armed with a shotgun, who ventured out beside the boulder. Hannah aired him out. "Uhgh," he grunted before taking a beach siesta. A third armed bad guy approached, and Chris smoke checked him. Each of these men were in the photos that Willy had sent. It seemed as if tonight the whole Russian mafia crew was out on the beach.

Hannah fired again, but from Chris's angle, he couldn't see who she was shooting at. Whoever he was, he didn't shoot back.

Chris turned the corner and spotted a man with a shotgun and a gleam in his eyes, but before the man could squeeze off a shot, Chris put him down.

Chris needed to clear the area behind the nearest boulder, but a tattooed man emerged from the back door, and Chris unloaded on him instead. The first shots struck Tattoo in the chest, but Chris's follow-up shot missed.

Meanwhile, a heavy-duty guy turned the opposite corner of the house, but Chris had to finish off Tattoo. Rather than go for the more difficult head shot, Chris lazed Tattoo's chest and put three more shots into it. Tattoo dumped on his duff as if he couldn't wait to sit. Then his body stiffened, and he toppled over.

Heavy D got off two shots in Hannah's direction. Without sound suppression, the shots sounded like thunder echoing off the cliff walls. Hannah's *tick-tick* answered Heavy D. Chris added his laser to Heavy D's upper body and jerked the trigger rapidly. Heavy D plummeted. Chris shot him some more to make sure he stayed put.

He turned to check on Hannah. She lay on her side with one leg folded under, and she didn't move. The side of her head leaked profusely.

"Man down," Chris whispered. He knelt. Hannah's eyes were closed, and she didn't make a sound.

He didn't want to believe she was dead. He felt the artery on her neck for a pulse. A gentle throbbing pulsated against his fingers. *She's alive!* He put his cheek near her mouth to feel for breathing and watched her chest for a rise and fall. Her chest didn't move, but air from her nose tickled his skin. She was breathing. Even so, her eyes remained closed and her body still. "We need to medevac Infidel."

Max's voice came over the radio. "Leave Infidel there, grab the HVT, and we'll take Infidel out with us."

Chris unpacked a dressing from the blowout kit on her dive belt and affixed it to her wound. "I'm taking her out now."

"Don't abandon us," Max said. "We need to get the HVT."

Chris heard Max's words, but he was so focused on saving Hannah that he couldn't process their meaning. "Bradley, Reverend. Need immediate extract."

"Okay," Angelo said.

One of the Russians from Willy's photos, Godzilla with no neck, rushed out of the back door pointing his shotgun. Chris aligned his laser and pulled the naked steel trigger so fast that it seemed he was firing on full auto. Godzilla did a dirt dive.

Chris shifted his FN P90 on its sling to his back and his attention to Hannah. He picked her up. She was no lightweight, but he was filled with more strength than he imagined possible. He loved her, and he wasn't going to let her die. He carried her into the ocean.

Her eyes popped open, she snorted, and her body twitched as if the cool saltwater brought her back to consciousness.

The water's buoyancy made her lighter, and he popped the compressed air cartridge on her inflatable life vest. Soon she was floating without his help. Chris put on his swim fins. He kicked like a madman and distanced himself from the Russians. Farther and farther he swam out to sea.

The faint murmur of the yacht increased in volume.

Chris swam harder, and he barely had enough breath to speak: "Bradley, I hear you. I'll signal, you identify."

"Okay."

On the back neck area of Hannah's vest was attached an unused glow stick. Chris bent it until the thin glass capsule inside broke, releasing its solution into the surrounding chemicals and casting an infrared glow.

"I see a red IR light," Angelo said.

"That's correct. We need an extract, ASAP."

The engines hummed, and the dark vessel materialized from the night. "Engines stopped," Angelo said. The engines continued to idle, but the yacht stopped moving.

Chris swam Hannah closer to the stern, where Angelo met them. Chris pushed her up and Angelo pulled until she was aboard. Then Chris kicked himself up out of the water and pulled himself onto the deck. Angelo hastily returned to the helm and got them moving again.

Chris jerked off his fins and dropped them on the deck. He picked Hannah up and carried her across the sundeck to the multi-cushioned sofa-bed, where he laid her.

Her eyes were closed.

Chris sat beside her and took off his night vision goggles. The emerald world surrendered to the real world. "You're going to be okay," he said.

Hannah stirred and opened her eyes—they were dilated. "Dad?"

"What?" Chris asked gently.

She closed her eyes again.

The yacht pulled forward to full speed, and the glowing lights on the mountainside glided past. Chris unzipped Hannah's wetsuit partway to relieve some of the pressure on her chest and help her breathe more easily. He had no romantic thoughts now, his only focus was her survival.

She opened her eyes and sat up. "What's going on? Why aren't we attacking the objective?"

"We did. You were injured."

Her body swayed unsteadily. "We did? Did we get Doctor Kuznetsov?"

"I don't know. You need to rest."

"I'm fine," Hannah said.

"Do you remember what happened?"

"What?"

"You were shot—the bullet grazed you or a ricochet hit you. You passed out and your head was bleeding."

"Where are we going?" she asked.

"The hospital."

"I'm fine. We need to snatch the doctor."

Chris became impatient. "You were seriously injured—you might have a skull fracture. Your brain could be bleeding or infected. We need to get you to the hospital. Make sure you're okay."

"What about Max and Tom?"

"I told them I was medevac'ing you. They're big boys—they can make big boy decisions." Chris put his arm around her. "You need to lie down and rest."

The urgency in her voice faded, and she sounded as if she were talking in her sleep: "I'm okay." She almost fell over, but Chris eased her down, and she closed her eyes—in a happy place.

Riding across the Bay of Naples with her brought him back to a day several months before, floating on the Tidal Basin in Washington, DC, when he asked her the question. She was a busy woman, but he felt blessed that she spent much of the little free time she had with him. He stopped their white swan boat rental on the water within view of the Jefferson Memorial. Spring's morning sun glinted off the gleaming white dome of the pantheon, its steps descending into the water. On the other side, cherry blossoms popped like popcorn. The popcorn poured into Potomac Park, laying down a carpet of dazzling white. There were other people in the park and on the water, but Chris and Hannah were in their own little world.

Hannah had the curves of *une belle* and the heart of a warrior. Smiling didn't come easy for Chris, but it came easy for her. When they were alone like this, it was the serenity in her cocoa-colored eyes that comforted him.

He put his arm around her.

She softly leaned into him. "I thought we were just friends."

Chris smiled. "This is a friendly arm."

Like the blooming of the cherry blossoms and this moment with her, blissful moments came and went like dreams, and before the dream evaporated, he leaned over to kiss her, but she kissed him first.

"I thought we were just friends," he teased.

"That was a friendly kiss."

Then the question came to him. He'd thought it many times before, but this time the feeling came so hard and so fast that he couldn't avoid it any longer. And there was the small chance she might say "yes."

"Will you marry me?" he asked. "I'd go to Hell and back for you."

"You already have. More than once."

Chris lowered his gaze. "But you won't marry me."

"I'm not a good fit for you," she said kindly.

Chris's heart ached. "I don't understand."

She sighed, and her face became more serious. "I'm already married."

Chris was shocked.

"To my work," she explained.

Chris's nerves settled down. "I know."

"We don't get that much time together," she said.

"And I'm okay with that. Is it because I'm—you know?"

"No, it's not because you're a preacher."

He confronted the possibility that he didn't want to confront. "You don't love me."

She took a deep breath.

Chris waited.

"Father was a CIA officer who went missing in action before I ever knew him," Hannah said. "Mother gave me his picture—it was her most prized possession. More than once she said that Father and I had the same eyes, and the picture seemed to confirm it. In his absence, Mother sometimes played music from his personal collection. She said that 'Another One Bites the Dust' was his favorite.

"I remember when I was little—a weekend before Father's Day. Mother and I had gone shopping at the supermarket. As I often did, I looked for my father's face, but none of the other shoppers or grocery store employees were him. I passed the vegetables and meat section, and I imagined him grilling vegetables and steaks on a barbeque for Mother and me. In the frozen food aisle, I thought about an evening with him on the sofa, watching TV and eating ice cream.

"While Mother searched for shampoo, I drifted into the greeting cards section. There seemed to be so many cards for so many occasions, even graduation. I envisioned Father attending mine one day. There were Father's Day cards, and I opened one and read the words inside. Another girl joined me and did the same. After we'd read several, a man appeared in the aisle. 'There you are,' he said with a smile. 'I was looking for you.' For a moment, I thought he was talking to me. I was so happy—like I'd never been happy before. But he held the other girl's hand and led her away. I felt embarrassed, small—lost and alone. More than the barbeque or ice cream—or greeting card—all I wanted in the whole world was a hug from my father. As a child, Father's Day always cut like a knife through the gut."

Tears flowed from Hannah's eyes. "If I were to marry you—then lose you—I couldn't bear to suffer like that again."

Chris appreciated that in private; she'd always been open with him. He wiped away her tears. "I didn't know." He felt sorry for her—and he felt sorry for himself. Part of him wanted to dig a hole and bury his love for her. But another part of him didn't want to give up. In light of the situation, he chose to simply be satisfied with her friendship.

Chapter Twenty

Following urgent orders from "the Center," FSB headquarters, Minotaur flew under diplomatic cover from Syria to the Embassy of the Russian Federation in Sofia, Bulgaria. The Center didn't say why; they simply told him to go to Bulgaria and await further orders.

At noon, he swam in the embassy's four-lane, short-course pool—half the length of a fifty-meter Olympic-size pool. Although the air temperature hovered around seventy degrees, the pool was heated. He swam to stay fit, but he also swam to forget the countersniper mission that he left Bear to wrap up. The water lifted the weight of his unfinished business.

Two fully clothed young men marched out onto the pool deck and halted at the shallow end of the pool. One of them pointed at Minotaur. He stroked to the shallow end, stopped, and stood facing them.

"*Minotavr?*" the smaller one asked in Russian.

"*Da,*" Minotaur replied. *Yes.*

"We were told to escort you to Semyon Nikolaevich." Both lower ranking and upper ranking Russians addressed each other by their given name and patronymic name—except for special officers like Minotaur, who went by their code names.

Minotaur pulled himself up onto the deck and strolled into the pool house. The two young men followed him inside, where they averted their eyes while he changed out of his swim shorts and dumped them in a duffel bag. He threw on undershorts and concealed an MP-443 Grach pistol in an abdomen holster under his trousers. Near the turn of the millennium, he and a handful of comrades like Bear received the newly completed Grachs before anyone else, and now they still held on to them. Owning one of the originals was a badge of honor, and they were good weapons, too. In his line of work overseas, he had to hide his identity and couldn't carry a Russian weapon, but here at the Russian Embassy in Bulgaria it was different. It was like home.

He put on his shirt, which he left untucked to help hide the Grach. Then he put on his socks and shoes, picked up his duffel bag, and approached the men. They guided him out of the dressing room, across the sprawling compound, and past the soccer green, clay tennis court, grove of trees, and various buildings to "Porcupine," a skyscraper topped with an array of antennas and satellite dishes.

Porcupine's security guard at the front entrance waved them through, and Minotaur let his two young escorts precede him down into the basement. He imagined drawing his weapon and shooting each of them in the back of the head. First he visualized himself actually doing it—internal imagery. Then he watched himself shoot them as if watching a YouTube video—external imagery. The better he could imagine such acts, the more skillfully he could execute them in real life. Of course real practice and actual experience were critical, too. *Praktika delayet sovershennym.* Practice makes perfect.

Inside Porcupine sat the prison cell. Although Minotaur couldn't see the jail from the hallway, he was aware of its presence, and his respiration pumped like pistons. He held his hands near his abdomen, close to his pistol. This could be an ambush. It wasn't likely, but anything was possible.

The two men ushered Minotaur into a conference room with soundproof walls, a concrete floor, and a little old man who sat at the opposite end of a table. Minotaur immediately recognized him as Semyon Nikolaevich, chief of Spetsgruppa "A," Special Group "A." He must've just flown in from Moscow. Minotaur hoped the news was good, but more often than not, the news was bad, so he steeled himself for the worst.

Semyon Nikolaevich had no papers or electronic devices in front of him. Like other FSB officers, he prided himself on his memory and rarely sent or received dispatches. "Please, sit," he said.

Minotaur parked himself in a chair.

Semyon Nikolaevich offered a cigar. "You did a fine job in Turkey."

Minotaur took one. The checkered band with raised gold lettering marked it as a Cuban Cohiba, the same that the late Cuban dictator, Fidel Castro, smoked. "Thank you."

Semyon Nikolaevich took a cigarette lighter out of his pocket and opened it. He lit Minotaur's cigar and then his. "And you are legendary in our community for assassinating the Ukrainian commander in Kiev."

Minotaur's cigar tasted full and peppery. "Russia was simply trying to host the Olympics in Sochi, but the West had to tarnish the moment by inciting Ukrainians to protest Russia. The Ukrainian commander was a puppet of the West. I only wish I could've killed him earlier."

Semyon Nikolaevich blew smoke high into the air. "The West does whatever it wants. If it doesn't like a leader, it replaces him—same as they did in Libya to Muammar Gaddafi and in Iraq to Saddam Hussein."

"Yes, the West is out of control. It's our responsibility to rein them in."

Semyon Nikolaevich nodded. "*Some* would-be assassins are—how shall I say—committed enough to make the kill, but they lack the calmness to avoid detection. If they are not discovered before they complete their mission, they will certainly be discovered after. *Other* would-be assassins are so calm and careful that they lack the energy and risk-taking to get the job done. But you are neither. You possess both the correct faculties to get the job done and the necessary composure to escape."

"It's generous of you to say so."

"Even so—"

Minotaur lowered his cigar and became still. *Uh-oh, here it comes.* He had to remind himself to breathe.

"Well," Semyon Nikolaevich continued, "your Ukraine operation was some time ago, and Ukraine continues to be a thorn in Moscow's side. Now, there's another issue." He looked gravely at Minotaur, seeming to weigh in his mind how to approach a delicate matter. "Pope Francis's support of the Catholic Church in Ukraine is making the whole situation worse. The Vatican has condemned our interests in Ukraine and publicly spoken against Russian involvement. The power of the papacy has gone to his head."

Minotaur had no opinion on the matter. Politics wasn't his business, killing was. He simply agreed with his boss on political matters: "Clearly."

"I am told you've been briefed on our new viral weapon, BK-16."

Minotaur nodded.

"The perfect drug to eliminate the pope. What you may not know is that first we tested it out on some low-level subjects. Then we did a major operational test of the virus—the assassination of CIA's chief of station in Turkey, William Hart. Hart was supporting the overthrow of our ally in Syria, President Assad. We assigned a man, codenamed Falcon, to deal with Hart. Falcon didn't know he was working for us. He succeeded in infecting Hart, but Falcon was captured—probably by CIA. Hart is now hospitalized and in serious condition. We expect he will be dead soon."

"Excellent," Minotaur said. "But I don't understand why you're telling me this. I was in the middle of a mission to kill a countersniper and his partner."

"I read your report. You stated that a militia-clan leader named Azrael poisoned them with BK-16. I know you're trying to hunt these two down—see to it personally that the job is finished—but now that is not necessary. They'll be dead soon enough. I need you for something more urgent. I am assigning you to terminate the pope from the papacy."

Minotaur was disappointed to be pulled off the Syrian countersniper mission before he tied up loose ends; however, the excitement of assassinating the pope more than made up for it. He wanted to keep his emotions in check, so he puffed on his cigar. He also wanted to confirm what he thought he'd heard. "Terminate Pope Francis."

"He has shown us no courtesy—acting beyond the limits of acceptable human behavior. And he continues to do so."

"Terminate with extreme prejudice?"

"Yes." Semyon Nikolaevich tapped his cigar ashes onto the floor. "I want you to use BK-16 for the job. You will fly to Rome and meet an Italian-Russian FSB officer named Mikhail Aleskeevich—he goes by Michael." Semyon Nikolaevich showed Minotaur a picture of a man who looked like an Al Pacino in his early thirties. "This is him."

"The bona fides?" Minotaur asked.

Semyon Nikolaevich described what Michael would be wearing and the prearranged words they were to exchange.

Minotaur nodded. He had a photographic memory and didn't need to be told twice. "How much support will I have?"

"How much do you need?"

"I need Bear. And four men for additional muscle, preferably locals, so they blend in. And we may require additional supplies and support from the Rezident in Rome."

"I thought you might choose Bear—excellent choice. I'll see to it about the others and contact the Rezident." Semyon Nikolaevich handed him two Bulgarian passports.

Minotaur examined them. One had his photo and alias, and the other had Bear's. Bulgarians were allowed travel without a visa to Italy and other member countries of the European Union.

"Michael will drive you to meet with Dr. Nastya Rossi, who will give you a vial containing the virus. Five days after administering BK-16 to the pope, he will expire. After that, I want you to stay out of Western Europe for at least a year." Nikolaevich paused, then said, "You understand that this mission does not exist, nor will it ever exist."

"I understand." Minotaur feared failure like he'd never feared failure before. He wasn't scared of Semyon Nikolaevich or death. Rather, it was as if his whole life had prepared him for this moment, and he didn't want to let himself down.

But instead of crippling or paralyzing him, his fear energized him.

Chapter Twenty-One

We only have two days to live, Max thought. He'd always figured that if he knew how many days he had to live, he'd spend them whooping it up with women, food, and booze, but the reality was that he was spending them finding an antidote to save his brother. And he was okay with that.

On the lower deck of their yacht in the marina, he finished cleaning the wound on his shoulder and bandaging it again. Fortunately the gunshot from the raid hadn't been a direct hit—the bullet just grazed him. Anxiously, he walked over and stared at the door to the guest head where their prisoner, Doctor Kuznetsov, was being kept on ice. Tom stood beside Max.

"Think he'll be ready to talk this time?" Max asked.

"Hope so."

Max opened the door. The head was the size of one in a commercial airplane, with a sink, toilet, and barely enough space for two people. The toilet seat was down and Doctor Kuznetsov sat on it making a noise that sounded like sobbing, but it was difficult to tell with the gag in his mouth and the hood covering him. The noise-cancelling earphones prevented him from hearing Max's arrival, and Max announced his presence with a punch to the face—not enough to kill him, or even knock him out, but enough to get his attention. The doctor jerked backwards and bounced his noggin off the bulkhead. Then he balled up into a defensive position.

"What're you doing?!" Tom asked.

"Softening him up."

"Is that necessary?"

Max didn't like being second-guessed by his younger brother, so he blew it off.

"Can we ask him the questions without the drama?" Tom asked.

Max frowned and removed the earphones.

The doctor recoiled.

Next, Max removed the hood and gag. "We need an antidote for BK-16," Max said.

"Yes," Doctor Kuznetsov said. His composure indicated he was eager to cooperate. "I know another scientist who has the antidote. If she does not have it, she can make it. She is the same person who created BK-16."

"I thought you made BK-16."

"She is a junior scientist, and I am a senior scientist, so she does the work."

"And you take the credit," Tom said.

The doctor shielded his face with his hands.

"What's her name?" Max asked.

"Nastya Rossi," the doctor said. "An Italian-Russian."

"Where?" Max asked.

"Rome. She lives on Viale Citta d'Europa."

Footsteps sounded on the deck above, and there were voices. Max speedily gagged the doctor, put on his hood and headphones, and shut him in the guest head again.

"Who is it?" Tom whispered.

"Hope it's Chris and not the cops," Max said. He rushed to the foot of the stairs and looked up. On the main deck, a figure approached. Then he came down the steps. It was Chris.

"How's Hannah?" Max asked.

"She caught a ricochet to the head, and it knocked her out for a couple minutes or so. She still can't remember the Russians we whacked at Doctor Kuznetsov's hideout or me getting her on the boat, but she seems to remember everything else. The doc says she'll be fine, but she needs some rest. He's going to do some more tests."

"I'm glad she's okay," Tom said.

"Did you get Kuznetsov?" Chris asked.

Max pointed to the guest head. "In there."

"Yes!" Chris smiled and put out his fist for a fist-bump, but Max left him hanging.

"You abandoned us," Max said.

"I'm sorry."

Max's voice became tense. "We almost died in Sorrento because of you."

Chris raised his head. "But you're alive, and you snatched the HVT."

"I thought preachers were supposed to help out their neighbor and all that," Max said. "Not be assholes."

"If you were me, and it was your brother Tom instead of Hannah, would you have left him on the ground and continued the mission?"

Max pondered his words.

"That's what I thought," Chris said.

Max didn't back down. "Why didn't God take care of Hannah—so you could help the rest of your teammates?"

"I don't know," Chris said.

"Why doesn't God stop this BK-16? How many more people need to die before He lifts a damn finger? How many more massacres or genocides in the world?"

"The Lord works—"

"If you say 'in mysterious ways,' I'll kick your Bible-thumping ass."

Chris raised his hands and looked away.

Tom cleared his throat. "The doctor who created BK-16 is in Rome. She might have an antidote. If not, she can make it. We should get going."

Chris turned to Tom and asked, "We driving there?"

"What about all our weapons and stuff on the boat?" Tom asked. "Do we have a safe house in Rome?"

Max exhaled as if blowing off steam. "Angelo could take us on the yacht to the outskirts of Rome, and this could continue to be our safe house."

"We'll need vehicles to get around on land," Tom said. "One of us could drive up the van or the sedan."

"Or maybe Angelo could get us a fresh vehicle in Rome," Max said.

"Fresh vehicle sounds good," Chris said.

"Let's ask Angelo," Max said.

The three of them climbed the stairs to the main deck and conferred with Angelo.

"*Nessun problema*," Angelo said.

"Does that mean 'there's a problem' or 'there isn't a problem'?" Max asked anxiously.

"No problem." Angelo got on his phone and texted.

Max looked out over the transom. The marina had boats but no people—except one. He carried a pair of big black bags and headed in Max's direction with the determined walk of a terrorist. "Who is this guy?" Max asked. There was something familiar about him that Max couldn't place, but it was too dark to see clearly.

"Sonny!" Chris exclaimed.

Sonny had no hair, a slight gut, and a whole lot of attitude. He sauntered across the gangplank and dropped his bags on the deck. "Did you miss me?"

Max was excited to see him again after their recent mission together in the German Alps. "Long time, no see."

Tom seemed less enthused. "Hi, Sonny."

"Where's Hannah?" Sonny asked.

"In the hospital," Chris said.

"In the hospital?" Sonny asked.

"She got knocked on the head," Chris said, "but she seems to be recovering."

Angelo rose to his feet. "Who's this?"

"I'm Sonny, King of Jews." Sonny held out his hand. "You may kneel and kiss my ring."

Angelo gave him a quizzical look, as if something was lost in translation. "I'm simply Angelo."

Chapter Twenty-Two

Max and his brother only had one more day to live—unless they found a cure. Angelo steered them along with Chris and Sonny north on the Tyrrhenian Sea, following the Italian coast. Max was topside when he felt something dribble from his nose. At first he thought he had a runny nose, but he wiped it with the back of his hand, and he discovered that it was blood. He thought it might be the effects of the BK-16, but he wasn't sure, and he didn't want to alarm his brother or the others, so he hid it. Even when he wasn't concerned about worrying others, out of habit, Max hid signs of pain or weakness.

Chris rose from below with steaming plates of omelets, hash browns, and toast. "Too late for midrats and too early for breakfast, but since everyone's awake, thought I'd make breakfast anyway." Midrats was short for midnight rations.

Max avoided eye contact and slipped past Chris while trying to hide any more blood that might seep out. "Go ahead and start without me," Max called out behind him, "but save me a plate." He descended the stairs, hastily stepped into the master head, and closed the door. More blood had gathered on his upper lip. He grabbed some toilet paper, wiped the blood, and tossed the evidence in the shitter. He bent over to grab the flushing handle, but he felt faint and had to grab the sink to prevent himself from taking a dive into the toilet bowl. *This must be the BK-16.* He hit the handle and flushed. Still feeling light-headed and afraid he might fall in, he lowered the lid. Then he washed his hands and face to help him stay conscious. He sat on the toilet. There he remained for several minutes. Gradually, his strength returned.

He exited the head and climbed the stairs, but he felt like he was only operating on two-thirds of his strength. When he arrived topside, everyone was eating.

Sonny eyed Max's plate. "You want your omelet?"

Max ignored Sonny, took a seat, and dug into his food.

Sonny turned to Chris and complained, "You didn't make coffee."

Chris drank a swig of his orange juice. "I don't drink coffee."

Sonny looked to Tom as if soliciting support. "Tom drinks coffee."

Tom shook his head. "Not this morning, thanks."

"Doesn't anyone on this boat want coffee?" Sonny lamented.

"I do." Max stuffed his mouth with omelet.

With one hand, Angelo steered them along the Mediterranean Sea and with the other he ate a forkful of hash browns. "I like coffee."

Sonny stood. "Don't everyone jump up at once to make it. You guys are as useless as condom machines in the Vatican." He stormed below, and a clatter sounded from the galley.

Angelo chuckled.

"Angelo, are you Catholic?" Tom asked.

"Yep."

"Max and I are, too," Tom said.

Max grunted. "Was."

"I still am." Tom ate a piece of toast.

Chris pulled out his phone and made a call. "I'm calling to ask about a patient, Hannah Morton." Her real last name was Andrade—Morton was an alias. There was a long pause. "Do you know what happened to her?" Then there was another pause. "Thank you." Chris ended the call and put his phone in his pocket.

"Is she okay?" Max asked.

Chris didn't seem happy. "She's not there. Soon after I dropped her off, she must've left without checking out."

Tom continued to nibble on his toast. "Why?"

"She hates hospitals," Chris said, "and she wants to be where the action is. I understand, but I wish she'd have stayed put—given herself more time to recover."

Max liked the idea of seeing her again, and she was a useful addition to the team. "You think she's coming here?"

"Where else would she go?" Chris asked.

"Does she know where we are?"

"I messaged Willy with an update on our status," Max said. "All Hannah has to do is ask him."

Sonny returned with a cup of mud and sat.

Max could see that Sonny's service didn't extend to him, so he walked down to the galley, poured two cups of brew, and returned to the upper deck. He gave one to Angelo before joining the others at the table.

"We need to discuss how we want to set up surveillance on Dr. Nasty's apartment in Rome," Max said. Since working for CIA's SAD/SOG (Special Activities Division/Special Operations Group) he was used to doing more with less, and having a four-man team was a welcome luxury.

Sonny swallowed a bite of hash browns. "We'll take a look, and as soon as the opportunity presents itself, we'll snatch the doctor."

They discussed the details of the mission while they finished breakfast.

⸺⬤⸺

THE SKY TURNED THE sky's dimmer switch from black to gray, and planes ascended and descended the sky over Leonardo Da Vinci International Airport. Max and the others cruised past a pair of sailboats on the Mediterranean. Farther north floated a dozen or so fishing boats. Angelo pulled into a wharf where hundreds of pleasure craft were docked.

Max went aft and hung out boat fenders so the yacht wouldn't scrape against the dock, while Angelo found a parking spot and backed up to a pier.

Tom stood by to jump out and help tie up the lines to the dock, but Sonny put a hand on his shoulder and said, "Let the squids handle this," using the pejorative word for Navy sailors. Like Tom, Sonny had been an Army Ranger. Unlike Tom, Sonny earned a slot on Delta Force, the Army's tier one unit, similar to the Navy's SEAL Team Six. Sonny was still in the Army, but now he was "on loan" to CIA for this mission.

Max and Chris hopped out of the yacht and tied the vessel to the pier.

A young man with curly black hair and wearing a suit stood on the pier next to a gray midsize crossover SUV—in the States it was a Dodge Journey, but here in Rome, the SUV was marked Fiat.

"That's our ride," Angelo said. He went ashore and talked with the man.

The young man in the suit gave Angelo a set of keys, exchanged some words, and left.

Angelo returned and handed the keys to Max. "These are to the Fiat Freemont."

"Thanks." Max tossed the keys to Tom.

"What should I do with the prisoner while you guys are ashore?" Angelo asked.

"Just keep him here until we can verify the intel about the scientist," Max said.

Tom went ashore, got behind the wheel of the SUV, and started the engine. Max, Chris, and Sonny loaded into the vehicle, too. Then Tom shifted into drive and used the GPS on his phone to navigate. They rode through the outskirts of Rome.

After twenty-three klicks, Tom parked on the shoulder of the road, leaving a few open spaces between their SUV and the other vehicles parked there. In front of them were two hundred meters of manicured grass bordered with trees—a park. To the right of that was Dr. Rossi's tan and ivory seven-story apartment building and four more apartment buildings similar to it. Across the street from the apartment were high rises filled with shops and restaurants.

"We might make a scene if we go direct action to get Dr. Rossi," Tom said.

Sonny groaned: "Here comes the good idea fairy."

"I agree with Tom," Chris said.

"Great," Sonny said sarcastically.

"What do you have in mind, Chris?" Max asked.

"Break down the door, bag, and drag her," Sonny said.

"What if someone sees us?" Tom asked. "We've got no package delivery or utility uniforms."

"We could get some," Sonny said.

Max sighed. "That'll take time, valuable time."

"Too bad Hannah isn't here," Sonny said. "She could just go up there and talk to the woman."

"I could go up there and talk to her," Chris said.

"That's a stupid idea," Sonny said.

"It's your idea," Chris countered.

Sonny gave him the evil eye. "I said Hannah should go up there, not you."

"A minister is an expert in matters of the heart," Tom said. "If any of us could convince the scientist to help us, Chris could."

"Does she speak English?" Sonny asked.

"She's a scientist; she should at least speak a little," Chris said.

Max looked at his watch. It was 7:23 a.m. "Going soft will save us time without creating a scene. If she resists, we can take her down hard."

Tom nodded in agreement.

Sonny shook his head.

"I'll be back in a minute." Chris opened the door and strolled along an asphalt walkway toward the scientist's building.

There was a long silence. Chris's microphone transmitted only his voice through the vibrations in his neck—not his footsteps, a door opening, or anything like that.

Finally, Chris's voice transmitted: "I'm from a power that's here to help you. We need your help, too." That was his pitch. Then everything went quiet. He spoke again: "I understand your distrust of Doctor Kuznetsov and the FSB, but I'm not them. Far from it..."

She's not buying it, Max thought.

Chris's voice returned. "I'm from a greater power than that... What is it you really need?" There was a long pause. It was only seconds, but it seemed like minutes. "Yes, I can get you out of here and take you anywhere you want... If you have an antidote for BK-16, we need it; if you don't, we'd like you to make it. People have already been killed by it, and more will die if you don't help us... Is this what you became a scientist for?"

There was another long pause.

"Come on," Sonny said. "Enough talk, let's take her!"

"How much time do you need?" Chris asked. "Ten minutes is good... I'm Chris..."

Although Max understood that the doctor would be out of her house in ten minutes, fifteen minutes passed, and there was no sign of Chris or the scientist. They could be in trouble.

Max transmitted: "Reverend, everything okay?"

Squelch broke twice: *affirmative*.

Five more minutes passed...

"What's taking so long?" Max asked.

"Moving," Chris's voice came back.

"'Bout damn time," Sonny grumbled.

Chris grunted—twice.

"I'm going in," Max said. "Sonny, you and Tom wait here."

"Hey," Sonny said.

Max unassed the truck and jogged across the walkway and into the building. The elevator was busy, and he didn't like elevators anyway, so he ran up the stairs. He stopped at the fifth floor, breathing heavily, and found the scientist, who he recognized from her picture. She stood outside her apartment with a suitcase on the deck and cradling a big brown cat with gently curving stripes and an *M* on its forehead. The scientist stared at the apartment door across from her, which was open.

Max drew his weapon and held it down at his side. He wanted to be ready if Chris was in trouble, but he didn't want to make a scene if this was a false alarm. Max entered the apartment, and lying on the floor was a rugged-looking man with the side of his head bashed in and blood on the carpet. Beside him stood Chris, who simply said, "Let's go."

Max returned his pistol to its holster and walked out of the apartment. Behind him, he could hear the clicking sounds of Chris locking the door and closing it. Max picked up the doctor's suitcase and carried it.

She seemed in shock, but she followed Max down the stairs. Chris brought up the rear, securing their six. They walked briskly out of the building. Max put her suitcase in the trunk of the SUV, and Chris helped her into the back seat. Then Max and Chris hopped in, too.

Tom shifted into gear and rolled out onto the road.

Max offered his hand to the scientist. "I'm Max."

She shook it. "Nastya."

Tom steered them around a curve. "Tom."

Sonny grumbled.

The cat pulled its ears back and growled at him.

"I've been hoping and praying for this moment," Nastya said. "Thank you."

"Who was the neighbor back there?" Max asked.

Nastya petted her cat. "My driver, but he's a Russian FSB officer whose main job seems to be to keep an eye on me."

"He was in the hall when Nastya and I came out of her apartment," Chris said. "I didn't want to shoot him and make noise, so I hit him in the neck with my pistol, knocking him back into his apartment. Then I finished him."

Max turned to Nastya and asked, "Do you have an antidote for BK-16?"

"Not on my person," she said. "There is some at the lab."

"Where's your lab?" Tom asked.

"Downtown, near the Colosseum."

"We should go to the lab, now," Max said.

"Let's get Nastya to safety first," Chris said. "Then, if we can't get the antidote at the lab, at least we'll have someone who can make the antidote."

Chapter Twenty-Three

M inotaur listened to the jet engines and peered out the window of the Alitalia plane to see Leonardo da Vinci International Airport emerge from the darkness. He turned to Bear and said, "I hate Rome—it's too crowded and too Catholic." The plane landed, and Minotaur and Bear disembarked.

Minotaur's suit reflected his minimalist style: solid dark gray, single-breasted, and no belt loops or belt. The greatest tailor in Bulgaria used fine Italian wool to make this suit efficient, handsome, and inconspicuous. Because he kept the same physical fitness, and his weight never varied more than plus or minus two kilograms, he could wear it as often as he wished. His sleeves were loose so they wouldn't restrict him in shooting or moving. He liked a white French shirt, eschewing the bulk and weight of cuff links; instead, he wore buttons. His light gray, silk necktie was a shade lighter than his suit. He used the same Silhouette sunglasses as NASA because they flowed freely without hinge screws, and their titanium frame was light, flexible, and durable. On his feet were black, leather, derby shoes with sleek, plain toes—more versatile for all occasions than the more formal Oxfords. The soles were customized with treads for more efficient movement. The remains of a dead apex predator, alligator skin, wrapped around his wrist and held time in the form of a Swiss International Watch Company Aquatimer—worth about four thousand dollars, he could barter it in an emergency. Minotaur was a sleek killing machine.

Like a gray shark, he swam in and around a mass of passengers in the terminal, but Bear marched straight through, brushing a few shoulders and deterring others from entering his path. The crowd thinned out, and Minotaur and Bear rejoined each other for a moment. Minotaur continued his earlier thought: "Deep down inside, the Romans must know there is no God. They know that the emperor wears no clothes, but they're afraid of saying so and being ostracized—so they bow down anyway. As for me, I'm not afraid."

Bear grinned.

They separated again to pass through immigration. At the counter, Minotaur showed his Bulgarian passport to a middle-aged man wearing glasses and a bored expression.

"What is the purpose of your visit?" the officer asked in English.

To kill your pope, Minotaur thought. He returned the bored look and answered in English, "Business."

"What is your final destination?"

"Rome."

"How long will you be staying?"

"Three weeks."

"Where will you be staying?"

"The Lifestyle Suites Rome."

The officer passed him through.

Minotaur strolled over to the luggage carousel, picked up his bag, and waited in line for customs. At the counter, a young woman in uniform asked, "Do you have anything to declare?"

"No," Minotaur said.

"Did you pack your own bag?"

"Yes."

"Open it, please."

Whether he had contraband or not, or whether he worried about being discovered or not, he projected Zen-like calm. In this moment, he carried no weapons or other illegal items. His contact would equip him, and if he needed more contraband, he could requisition it through the Russian embassy in Rome—the FSB's *rezidentura.* Minotaur graciously opened his suitcase.

The immigration officer rifled through his clothes, toiletries, and other mundane items before pushing the suitcase aside and speaking to the next traveler. Although Minotaur appreciated her being timely, he wasn't happy at her disrespectful attitude and how she crumpled up his carefully folded clothes. He didn't want to linger near Italian authorities any more than necessary, so he closed the suitcase without ordering the messed up contents and departed.

Outside immigration, Minotaur met up with Bear and they proceeded through the waiting area, where they met a man who wore a red shirt and looked like a young Al Pacino. He greeted them in English. "Welcome to Italy."

Minotaur spoke English, too. "You our ride?"

"Yes, come with me."

"Excellent."

The brief exchange seemed natural, but the conversation was made up of pre-arranged bona fides to ensure that Minotaur met the person he was supposed to meet.

Michael escorted them through the airport.

"I understand there was some trouble in Sorrento," Minotaur said.

Michael guided them outside to a gray Mercedes-Benz Vito with black windows, sitting curbside with the engine running. "Yes. We've prepared as you instructed—to avoid future troubles." He opened the side door of the van, and they got in.

Five Italians were seated—two in front and three in back. All except the driver carried short-barreled Heckler & Koch 416s, German assault rifles similar to the American Colt M4. On the deck in the middle row were two more HK 416s. Michael closed the door and propped one of the rifles between his legs with the barrel aimed at the deck.

Minotaur grabbed one and briefly examined it before resting it between his legs.

Michael pointed to a pair of bulging duffel bags on the floor and said, "Those are for you, gentlemen."

Bear reached into the bag nearest him and pulled out a Serbu Super Shorty Remington 870 shotgun and swing-out holster. Then he took off his suit jacket and armed himself. In his bag, Minotaur found a Glock 19 pistol with an inside-the-waistband holster, a sound suppressor that appeared to screw onto the barrel of the Glock, and magazine pouches loaded with ammo. He put on the pistol and ammo and pocketed the silencer.

"Let's pick up the BK-16," Minotaur said.

"Now?" Michael asked.

Minotaur loaded a round in the chamber of his rifle. "Now."

Chapter Twenty-Four

A taxi stopped on the pier. *Who is this?* Max thought as he and the others escorted Dr. Rossi onto the Pershing yacht. Max's shoulders and arms tensed, and he moved his hands to the front of his abdomen so they'd be close to his concealed pistol in order to draw it speedily.

Hannah stepped out of the taxi.

Max's shoulders and arms relaxed. He waved to her, and she waved back.

Chris left them and walked aft to meet her. His voice lacked enthusiasm: "Welcome back."

"Thanks," she said. "What's wrong?"

"Nothing," he said.

"It sounds like something," she persisted.

"I just wish you would've taken more time to recover."

"Time we don't have," she said. "Willy told me where to find you."

"How you feeling?"

"Fine."

Chris and Hannah walked over to the pilothouse and joined the others.

Angelo, perched in his pilot seat, turned to face her. "Welcome back."

"Thanks, Angelo," she said.

Chris sat with Sonny, Max, Tom, and Dr. Rossi on the white leather couch that wrapped around the foldup table.

Sonny smiled and gave her a friendly nod.

"Glad you're okay," Tom said.

Her countenance beamed. "I heard you guys got Doctor Kuznetsov."

"He's stashed below in the guestroom head," Max said proudly.

Hannah extended her hand to Dr. Rossi and said, "I'm Hannah."

"Pleased to meet you," the doctor said. "I'm Nastya."

"The scientist," Hannah said.

"Yes."

"Thank you for helping us."

"Thank you for saving me," Nastya said.

Hannah sat in the copilot's chair next to Angelo and faced the group. "I'm afraid I have some bad news," she said. "Bill Hart died."

Max's heart felt like it had shrunk—the death of the CIA chief in Turkey meant that his brother's death was imminent.

Tom lowered his head.

"We'll get the antidote," Hannah said. "Today."

Nastya pulled out a pen and asked Angelo, "Could I have a piece of paper?"

"Sure." He paused for a moment before he rifled through his newspaper, and pulled out an advertisement that was blank on the back. "Is this okay?"

She took it. "Yes, thank you." On the table in front of them, Nastya sketched what appeared to be the layout of a building.

Hannah pointed to the sketch. "What're you drawing there?"

At the top of the drawing she wrote: Lab. "I worked with a small international team of scientists to research pharmaceuticals—at least that was my cover. My team didn't know that they were helping me create a viral weapon. They didn't know that was the lab's main purpose."

"Why not make BK-16 in Russia where you can do whatever you want?" Max asked.

Dr. Rossi continued to draw rooms and label them while she talked: "Many of the best scientists live overseas, and they're suspicious of Russia and won't live there," she said. "It's easier for an Italian pharmaceuticals company that pays lots of money to recruit good people." She wrote Supply Room on one of the rooms. "When not many of my colleagues are around, I go to this supply room, where there's a hidden door that leads to a secret room. In the room, I weaponize the BK-16 and make its antidote. After I receive a call from the FSB, I go to the room, pick up the BK-16 and the antidote, and go out for coffee, where I discreetly hand it off to an FSB officer."

"How'd you get mixed up in all this?" Chris asked.

"I was the top PhD graduate at Lomonosov Moscow State University—I learned quickly, found new ways to answer old questions, and I worked hard. I was flattered by my prospective employers, and I thought I'd be working for a top international pharmaceuticals company based in Italy. It wasn't until later that I discovered they were FSB. When I talked about leaving, they made subtle threats. I hated lying to good people, looking over my shoulder, and working through lunches, evenings, weekends, and holidays—I tried to commit suicide but failed. I didn't believe in God, but I started praying. I thought there was no hope, but then you came."

Tom tilted his head to the side. "How many FSB officers are in the lab?"

"At least two who I know of, maybe more," she said.

"Do you store the antidote in the secret room?" Max asked.

"Yes," she said. "The antidote is kept in titanium vials in storage."

"All right then, we go to the lab and snatch the antidote," Max said.

"If we enter from the back," Chris said, "we can get in and out a lot quicker."

"We should go in at night so we have fewer civilians to deal with," Sonny said.

Nastya rubbed at her hands. "Oh no."

Tom raised his eyebrows. "What?"

"An FSB officer is flying in today to pick up some BK-16 and antidote. Someone I haven't met before—his codename is Minotaur."

"What else do you know about this Minotaur?" Chris asked.

"An FSB officer told me that he's a gray-haired man wearing a gray suit who'll arrive in a gray Mercedes van. The officer seemed afraid of Minotaur."

"Do you know what time he's arriving?" Max asked.

"No, I just know he's arriving today."

"Alone?"

"I don't know."

Max stood. "We need to get the antidote before Minotaur does."

Hannah took out her cell phone. "I'll arrange for an asset to hold us a parking spot near the target. And I'll text Willy to pick up Nastya here and take her someplace nice and safe."

"I can text Willy about Nastya," Max said. "And while I'm putting him to work, I'll tell him to pick up our prisoner and take him someplace not so nice and not so safe."

Hannah flashed a mischievous grin. "Great." She turned to Angelo and said, "We'll need you to stay here until Willy sends someone to pick up Nastya and the prisoner."

Angelo nodded.

Chris turned to Hannah and asked, "You sure you're up to this?"

"Always," she said with a twinkle in her eye. "Assault rifles or submachine guns?" she asked.

"Sound-suppressed submachine guns will be quieter," Chris said.

"And lighter," Sonny said.

"Easier to conceal," Max added.

She looked at Tom as if to elicit a reply.

"Sound-suppressed submachine guns sound good," he said.

"Each of us can carry a blowout kit in the back left pocket," Max said, referring to the first aid kit. As per standard operating procedure, they didn't use their own blowout kit to patch up someone else because if they needed it later, they wouldn't have it, and the wounded person and his unused first aid kit could've already been medevaced out. The Good Samaritan who gave from his kit would be shit out of luck. This was why each team member carried a blowout kit in the same place so others could find it and patch up a wounded member with his or her own kit.

"Have any of you given shots before?" Nastya asked.

"Why do you ask?" Hannah asked.

She produced two wrapped syringes with needles. "You might need these."

Max took them and put one in Tom's left shirt pocket and one in his own. "What's the dosage for the antidote?" he asked.

"Fifteen milliliters," Nastya said.

Hannah flashed a wide smile. "Stellar. Meet back here with your gear in, say, twenty minutes?"

Max and the others nodded in agreement before separating to prep their kit. Max went below and put on a swing-out holster for his sound-suppressed FN P90 submachine gun. On the opposite side of his holster, he wore an extra fifty-round magazine in a custom-made pouch. Then he put a suit jacket on to conceal it. He also switched to a hip holster for his Glock, which would serve as a backup weapon.

He pocketed his blowout kit, and on his belt he strapped a smoke grenade and two flash-bangs. He thought of taking a fragmentation grenade instead of a flash-bang, but he figured there would be too many innocent civilians around to allow him a chance to use it without injuring them, so he stuck with the flash-bangs.

Twenty minutes later, the five operatives exited their lean and mean shark and stepped out onto the pier. The morning light glowed like a burning ember, illuminating jets coming and going like birds from the nest that was Leonardo Da Vinci International. With Max and his team on the prowl, the wild kingdom was about to get wilder.

Max rode shotgun in the Fiat SUV next to his brother. Chris, Hannah and Sonny jumped in behind them. Tom started the engine, drove to the Tiber River, and followed it for a klick and a half.

"I got a joke," Sonny said.

"Uh-oh," Chris said.

Max's ears perked up. "I want to hear it."

"Four guys are sitting on a bench in the park," Sonny said. "A black man, a Hispanic, a Jew, and a bigot. The black man notices that lying on the ground is an antique lamp from the Middle East. He picks it up and rubs it. A genie pops up and says, 'Wow, I've been in that lamp for ten thousand years. I'll give each of you whatever wish you want.' The genie looked at the black man and asked, 'What do you want?'

"'I want to go back to Africa and live in peace without poverty, and I want to take all my black brothers and sisters with me.'

"'Shazam, there you are,' the genie said. The black guy disappeared, and the genie turned to the Hispanic man and said, 'Next.'

"'I want to go back to Mexico with all my people and have good jobs and live in harmony,' the Hispanic man said.

"'Shazam. Next.'

The Hispanic man vanished.

The Jewish man looked amazed. "'I want to return to Israel with all my fellow Jewish people, and I want peace in the Middle East and no more terrorism.'

"'Shazam.' Then the genie turned to the bigot, who was all alone now, and asked, 'What is your wish?'

"'Let me get this straight, genie,' the bigot said. 'All the blacks are in Africa, all the Hispanics are in Mexico, and all the Jews are in Israel?'

"'Yes,' the genie said.

"'I'll have a Diet Coke.'"

Max and the others sat in silence.

"That wasn't funny," Tom said. "You're Jewish, Sonny. How can you joke like that about your own people? And others?"

Sonny shrugged his shoulders as if he couldn't care less.

"Sonny is offensive to everyone," Hannah said.

A moment later, something wet tickled Max's upper lip, and he surreptitiously wiped it away. It seemed like there was a jump in time, but he couldn't figure out why. *I must've drifted off—or passed out.* He looked to his left to see if anyone noticed. Tom sat beside him, driving with his eyes focused on the streets of Rome. Max glanced down at the thick liquid on his hand—blood, more than before. He wiped it on his pant leg. A wave of weakness washed over him, and he sat motionless, nervously waiting for it to pass. The streets of Rome blurred, and he blinked until his vision cleared. In the seat behind him, Chris, Hannah, and Sonny talked about something, but Max couldn't focus on it. He hoped he wouldn't become a liability on this op.

There was a sniffle—Tom.

"You okay?" Max asked.

"I'm good," Tom said.

Max suspected that the sniffle was blood and that his brother was hiding symptoms, too. They were running out of time to get the antidote.

Chapter Twenty-Five

Max's strength returned, and his urgency to get the antidote intensified. Using his thumb to peel up the side of his suit jacket, he clutched the handle of the pistol in his hip holster—but it didn't ease his worry.

Tom drove them into the heart of the city, and ancient ruins materialized. "We're a klick away from the lab."

The air became hotter, and Max wondered if he was developing a fever.

Sonny complained: "Is the A/C broken?"

Max moved the switch on the air cooler to High.

Ahead appeared the Colosseum. It was massive, standing about a hundred and fifty feet tall. Max had enjoyed the classic martial arts movie *Way of the Dragon*, where Bruce Lee and Chuck Norris fought each other to the death inside the Colosseum.

Tom steered through the downtown maze, found the target building, and parked. All except Tom got out of the SUV and climbed the metal stairs to the third floor, where they stacked up on the door. Hannah inserted the key, unlocked the door, and opened it.

BEHIND THE WHEEL OF their hacked Audi, Chris raced the team through the streets of Rome, Minotaur's gunmen in close pursuit. Hannah slumped in the back seat like her bones had become jelly. The car turned sharply, and she flopped into Max. "Hannah!" he shouted. There was a bloody gunshot wound in her left eyebrow and fragments of glass imbedded around it. She was one of those operators who he expected to be among the last survivors.

Chris took his eyes off the road. "Hannah!"

Max feared she was dead, but he hoped she was still alive. He touched her neck for a pulse, but there was none. Max shook his head.

A dull heaviness filled Max's skull, causing the world to tilt askew and colors to fade. A low-pitched tone hummed above all other sound. The heavy hum spread to his heart and his gut before it killed the feeling in his arms and legs. It was as if some dark force had pushed his soul out of his body. He couldn't feel Hannah's neck anymore, and he pulled his hand away.

Chris drove like a man possessed. "Hannah, wake up!"

Max felt sorry for Chris, but he deserved to know without ambiguity. "She's dead," Max said. "Hannah is dead."

"No, no, no," Chris repeated. The car slowed.

"What the hell, Max?!" Sonny shouted.

"Hannah saved my life while I was taking out the driver, but then she stopped firing. I don't know if she had sudden vertigo, tunnel vision, or what, but she stopped. And then she got hit. I think I nailed the gunman, but I was too late. I'm sorry."

Chris was exasperated and his voice weak. "I told her she needed more time in the hospital for that concussion."

The vehicle came to a halt.

Sonny reached over, put the SUV in park, and pulled Chris's arm. "You get in the passenger seat, and I'll drive."

For Max, seeing Chris's reaction to Hannah's death was like stepping back in time and seeing himself when his father died. Seeing Hannah die was horrible, but seeing Chris was worse, and Max turned away.

There was a wet blob of something on the floorboard, and Max didn't know if it was hair, or flesh, or bone, or brain, but it didn't belong there, and he didn't want Chris to see it, so he picked it up and searched Hannah's head for an exit wound. He found a small wet spot in the back of her head, and he attempted to stuff it back in.

Cars behind them honked, and people on the street slowed and stared.

Max said a silent prayer: *I know You and I haven't been on the best of terms for a long time. I'm not one to beg, but this is about my brother, and my friends, and I don't know what else to do. Don't know if you're even listening. But if you are and I've ever done anything good, please, keep Tommy and them alive. And please, don't let another of them die. At least not today. We've had enough for now.*

Chris had switched places with Sonny and sat in the front passenger seat. He spoke quietly and calmly, as if speaking in a direct stream of consciousness: "I'm going to kill Minotaur. Maybe not today, maybe not tomorrow, but I'm going to kill him."

Sonny stomped the accelerator, and their SUV leaped forward. Max resumed guarding their flank. Through the busted rear window, Rome receded in slow motion: mopeds and small cars were parked in front of *ristorantes* and *pizzerias*, and customers dined outside. Local landmarks passed through Max's view like disjointed snapshots: Leonardo da Vinci High School, a *farmacia*, and Carim Bank.

"I'm going to find us a parking garage where we can hide out for a minute and change vehicles," Sonny said.

They passed Centro Cavour Hotel, but there were no signs of a parking garage. On the opposite side of the street was a classical-style wall of concrete tagged with modern-day graffiti.

Max worried about his brother, so he radioed: "Tomahawk, you okay?"

No answer.

"Tomahawk, this is Yukon, come in, over."

"I'm okay," Tom said. "Trying to navigate these one-way streets. What's your twenty?"

Max looked around. "To our right is a church with twin domes and an over two hundred foot tall bell tower, each topped with a crucifix. On our left is the Argentinian Embassy."

"You're behind the Basilica di Santa Maria Maggiore," Tom said.

"We're traveling northwest on Torino."

"On my way," Tom said.

A couple hundred meters later, Sonny made a right and partway up the block he said, "There's a hotel." He drove clockwise around it. "The hotel next to it has parking."

Max whipped around to see the name of the hotel so he could tell Tom. "Tomahawk, go to Starhotels Metropole."

"Say again," Tom said.

"Starhotels Metropole. On Principe Amedeo Street."

There was a long pause. "Got it."

"Hope there isn't a valet," Sonny said.

"Or a parking attendant," Max said.

Sonny drove into the garage and stopped at a barricade. He took a ticket from a machine. The arm lifted, and he drove in. There were a number of vacant spaces—it was noon, and a lot of people must've checked out or were out for lunch. Sonny parked in a dim corner, and they waited.

Five minutes later, Tom rolled up and parked beside them. Max and Sonny stepped out of their vehicle, and Tom exited his.

Tom asked, "Is Hannah...?"

Max frowned and nodded.

Tom shook his head.

"Need you to pop the trunk," Sonny said.

Tom walked around to the back of his vehicle and opened the trunk.

Chris was the last one out. He half walked, half staggered, over to Hannah.

Max, Tom, and Sonny moved in to assist.

Chris dismissed them: "I've got this."

"We've got to help you," Tom said softly.

"I have it," Max said.

Chris struggled to look at her. "No."

Sonny grabbed Hannah's arm. "She's a part of us, too. Let us help."

Chris took the other arm. They pulled her out, and Max and Tom each took a foot. The four of them transferred her from the small Audi SUV to the cargo area of the larger Fiat SUV.

Chris stood there in a daze staring at her while the others grabbed Hannah's weapon and satchel out of the Audi and put them in the cargo area next to her. Max thought Chris would join them when they hopped inside the Fiat, but Chris just stood there gazing at her.

A pair of bearded men sauntered into the garage wearing black hoodies, T-shirts, and sunglasses, their sleeves pulled up to expose tattoos covering their flesh to the wrists. They headed in Chris's direction, their sagging pants hindering their forward momentum.

Chris must've sensed something because he turned and stared through them as if they were less than nothing. The two thugs sauntered like they were badasses in this neighborhood. Chris turned away from them in slow motion as if he didn't give them a second thought. Each of Chris's steps seemed filled with ennui. Without any sense of urgency or pausing to look back, he opened the door and crept into the truck. Gradually, he closed the door until it clicked shut.

Tom eased from the parking spot and rolled out of the garage. The two thugs bared their teeth and glared, as if pissed at being so easily dismissed. Max watched them through the rear window. Smaller and smaller, they shrank into insignificance.

Sitting in the back seat, Max reached forward into Tom's left shirt pocket and took the packet containing his syringe and needle. "Roll up your sleeve, I'm going to give you your shot."

"Shouldn't we send the antidote to CIA and make sure it isn't going to kill us before we inject it?" Tom asked.

Max looked in the rear cargo area and opened the satchel next to Hannah's body. He found a pair of green packs that looked like insulated lunch bags. He opened one. Inside were a dozen vials labeled *Anti-*

doto, cushioned like eggs in a carton. He hoped antidoto meant what it looked like it meant. He took one of the vials. "Bill Hart is already dead. We wait much longer, and it won't matter what we inject."

Tom stopped at a traffic light and rolled up his sleeve. "You take too many risks."

Max ripped off the packet from the needle and syringe. Then he placed the vial on the seat between his legs and removed the caps from the needle and vial. "Just keep us between the ditches, all right?"

Tom waited for the red light to change. "I don't want to attend your funeral. Dad's funeral was more than enough."

Max inserted the needle through the rubber top of the vial and into the drug and tugged the plunger back until he loaded fifteen milliliters into the barrel of the syringe. "You won't have to attend my funeral." He pulled the needle from the vial and thumped the syringe to make sure no air bubbles threw off his dosage. No bubbles.

"Sometimes I wish you would leave this world of black ops," Tom said.

Max sank the needle into Tom's shoulder muscle and pushed the plunger, injecting the antidote. "This world is all I know."

"This world is pain and tragedy. I only wish you could find someone and settle down."

Max put the cap back on the needle and returned it to Tom's shirt pocket. "There's nobody for me."

The light turned green, and Tom tapped the accelerator. "I only want you to be happy."

Max produced his own syringe with needle, loaded it from the same vial, and gave himself a shot. "Happiness and misery are best friends."

From the hotel parking garage, they drove half an hour through Rome. Tom steered onto the A90 Motorway, which circled Rome, but they'd hardly traveled several hundred meters of the circle before they slowed.

"Tommy, you okay?" Max asked.

Tom said nothing. There were no shoulders on the motorway to speak of, but Tom stopped in what appeared to be an emergency lane, painted with white chevrons and the letters SOS. From Max's angle in the back seat, he could see that at least one of Tom's eyes was shut. Max positioned himself to take a better look using the rearview mirror. Both of Tom's eyes were closed, and blood streamed down from both nostrils.

Tom didn't respond.

Chris stared at Max, who looked down at the front of his shirt. It was soaked in blood. He felt for bullet holes, but there were none. It had to be the BK-16. Or maybe the so-called antidote was actually poison. Max desperately wanted to say something, but all that came out of his mouth was one word: "Liechtenstein." The world went black.

WHEN MAX WOKE, SONNY was driving, and Tom was passed out in the front passenger seat. They were still on A90 Motorway, and there seemed to be no end to orbiting Rome, but it was preferable to being dead. Max felt as if he'd drifted out of his own body, but when he tried to return to his body, everything went black again...

Chapter Twenty-Six

Chris touched the artery in Max's neck—he could hardly feel it. Then he put his cheek near Max's mouth to feel for breathing.

Sonny continued to drive on the A90. "How's Max?"

"Pulse is weak and breathing shallow. We need to get him to a hospital ASAP." Chris moved forward in the SUV and checked Tom's pulse.

Sonny used his phone to navigate. "I'm exiting to A1 Motorway. We'll take a straight shot south to the naval hospital in Naples." The A1 was the spinal cord of Italy, connecting Milan in the north with Naples to the south and everything else in between, including Rome. "How's Tom?"

"Worse. I can barely feel his pulse or breathing." Chris returned to his seat.

Sonny switched to the far right lane and passed a barricade tagged with gang graffiti. A green sign ahead read: A1 Napoli. Sonny passed four dark compact cars. A sign showed a red circle with a white circle in the middle and the number forty, the speed limit in kilometers. The needle on the speedometer passed 60.

"I'm going to update Willy," Chris announced. He typed an encrypted text: we have the package. injected yukon and tomahawk, both in critical condition. en route rome to us naval hospital, naples. eta less than 2 hours. infidel dead. need pickup for package and infidel. Then he sent it.

He looked through the rear window to see if any suspicious vehicles were back there. A white tanker truck with a red diamond on the tank was the only vehicle to their immediate rear, and it dropped farther and farther behind.

Chris's eyes fell to Hannah, lying in the cargo area. He'd associated death with ugliness, but now he was surprised by how ethereally beautiful she was. She lived a life with few regrets, and it showed in her countenance. Her pink lips radiated like spring, and her perfume of vanilla and orange floated in the air. Her fairness caused his chest to burn and moved him to tears. He'd never known anyone like her, and he expected he'd never know anyone like her again. He silently swallowed his tears, but he choked and betrayed himself with sound.

"I miss her, too," Sonny said.

His tears continued to flow as he touched her cheek for the last time. It was as smooth as silk. He gently closed her eyes. *Rest.*

LESS THAN TWO HOURS after they departed Rome, they arrived at the US Naval Hospital in Naples. Chris wiped away his tears.

Hospital corpsmen met them at the emergency entrance with gurneys, and Chris and Sonny helped them put Max and Tom on the gurneys. The corpsmen wheeled the brothers away.

A different pair of corpsmen arrived, and Chris and Sonny assisted them in putting Hannah on a gurney. The corpsmen covered her with a white sheet before they scuttled away with her. Chris and Sonny wandered into the waiting room, where a nurse handed them some paperwork.

Sonny shook his head in disgust. Chris was too numb to react. Sonny filled out the paperwork before returning it.

Chris felt as if the batteries to his cell phone to God had died, and he needed to recharge them. "I'm going to visit the hospital chapel."

"I'll call Angelo," Sonny said.

"Meet you back here."

"Yeah."

Chris wandered through the hospital and found the chapel. The place was vacant, and he sat on one of the pews. There were no stained glass windows or crucifixes to remind him of God. It was a neutral room where Protestants, Catholics, Jews, Muslims, and others could fill it with their faith, but now Chris was the one who needed to be filled, and this place left him empty.

Rain came down, muffling the sounds of the city. Chris remembered when Hannah had come to see him in Dallas. It was clear skies when he took her out on the prairie, and they rode horses into the sunset. On the Fourth of July, they sat in lawn chairs near Addison Airport and watched stunt planes soar into the twilight's last gleaming. Fireworks glared red and other colors, and their sound burst in the air. They ate hot barbequed brisket and cold watermelon. Colors were more colorful and food more savory and sweet when he was with her.

During another visit, they sped down a hundred and thirty-two-foot long water slide called Tornado at Hurricane Harbor before retreating to his house and kissing in his pool as time stood still. When he visited her in the DC area, they hiked thousands of feet to the top of a peak in the Appalachians and sealed the summit with a kiss. At her house, they ate popcorn and binge-watched *The Walking Dead* on Netflix—their favorite character was a tie between sheriff's deputy Rick Grimes with his revolver and redneck Daryl Dixon with his crossbow; the black woman with the samurai sword, Michonne, came in at a close second. They agreed not to watch *TWD* alone until they could binge-watch together again. In the winter, they listened to live Christmas music while they gazed at the National Christmas Tree and rainbows of lights on conifers on the Ellipse in front of the White House. Another time when he flew out to see her, they went to the Smithsonian American Art Museum and viewed some of the most beautiful art he'd ever seen, but none of it could compare to her.

In one of the slots on the back of a bench was a Bible. He knew that reading it could charge his spiritual batteries, but it seemed a burden to walk over and pick it up, and even if he held it in his hands, he didn't think he could muster enough desire to read.

He needed to pray, but he couldn't. Ever since he was a child, he'd felt a special relationship with God, but the loss of Hannah seemed to indicate that that relationship might have changed. Chris wasn't angry at God—he'd never been so in his life, but he was sad in body, mind, and spirit. It reopened the wound of losing his childhood friend Nikkia, and it reopened the wounds of losing brothers in arms. On top of losing Hannah and the others, now it seemed he'd lost God, too.

Loneliness and fear gripped him. It felt like freefalling without a parachute, spinning aimlessly in black hopelessness. And all he could do was weep.

Chris sat there paralyzed with his grief and tears. He had to do something—anything. He may have fallen out of grace with God, but Reverend Luther was always a good friend and closer to God than any man Chris knew. He was Chris's mentor—and his inspiration.

Chris rubbed his tears away with his sleeve, took out his cell phone, and made the call. It was afternoon in Naples, but it was early morning in Dallas.

Reverend Luther answered. "Hello?"

"It's me."

"Chris? Is everything okay?"

"Not really," Chris said. "Hannah is dead."

"Oh no," Reverend Luther said. "I'm sorry. I'm so sorry."

Chris felt the tears come again, but he held them back. "I was calling for a couple friends of mine, Max and Tom. They're in real bad shape, and I was wondering if you'd pray for them."

"Of course I'll pray. I'll pray for you, too."

"Thank you."

"Is there anything in particular that you want me to pray for?" Reverend Luther asked.

Chris's blood ran cold. "The man responsible for killing Hannah—I want to kill him."

"Is it your job to kill him?"

"Doesn't matter. I'm going to do it anyway."

"Would it be possible to capture him alive?" Reverend Luther asked.

"Possible. But not likely."

"What if he surrenders?"

"No matter what he says, no matter what he does, I'm going to kill him."

"I'll pray for you to forgive him," Reverend Luther said. "When you can forgive him, you'll be able to focus on your job there—wherever you are. Then you can capture him dead or alive."

Chris thought for a moment, and he became angry. "I can *never* forgive him."

"You can. If you want to continue being a pastor, you must."

Reverend Luther demanded more of his congregation and Chris than other ministers, but the reverend gave more, too, and he was the gold standard of pastors. Chris had worked hard to live up to Reverend Luther's standards, but now he wasn't so sure he could do it anymore. An unseen weight pressed down on him, and he shrank under the burden of it all.

Chapter Twenty-Seven

Tuesday morning at the Russian Embassy, two klicks northeast of the Colosseum, Minotaur and Bear breezed into the office of the Rezident, Russia's chief spy in Rome. The Rezident, wearing a dark suit and tie, sat behind a large black desk, and in front of him sat a younger, thinner FSB officer wearing a dark suit, too. The Rezident stopped speaking, and the two looked at Minotaur.

"You can't come in here like this," the Rezident said.

Minotaur proceeded to the desk and stopped in front of it, standing beside the young officer. "I just did."

"Who do you think you are?" Rezident asked.

"I'm Minotaur. The Center sent me."

"I know that," the Rezident said. "You could have at least knocked."

Minotaur knocked on the desk and mustered a smile. "I need four to five pellets of ricin and a compressed air gun disguised as a camera." Minotaur didn't bother to explain to this self-important fool that two of the pellets were for testing the accuracy of the camera gun. The other two to three would be for the actual hit on the pope. He would act as if he were taking a picture when he shot the pope. The camera gun was no louder than a BB gun, and the sound of the crowd would drown out the noise of the shot. The pope would feel as if he'd been stung by a bee, but he and his security detail shouldn't suspect anything more serious than that.

"Everybody wants something," the Rezident said.

Minotaur stared through him. "I'm not everybody."

"You were supposed to pick up the BK-16 and use that. What's the matter?"

Now Minotaur was not happy. He wasn't angry, but he wasn't happy. "It wasn't there. And now I need your support. Didn't the Center tell you to support me?"

The Rezident opened his mouth as if about to say something, but his brain couldn't quite keep up. "Yes."

"I'm asking for your support—five pellets of ricin and a compressed air gun disguised as a camera to fire the pellets."

"We don't have that here."

Minotaur's body heat rose. "So get it."

"I'm not your lackey," Rezident said.

Minotaur strained to produce a smile. "Please."

Rezident folded his arms. He clung to the delusion that he had operational authority over Minotaur, which couldn't be further from the truth.

The younger man in the chair sat stiff as a wooden fence.

Minotaur pulled a sound suppressor out of his pocket with one hand and a pistol from his holster with the other. Then he screwed the suppressor onto the barrel.

Rezident stared at him dumbfounded, as if he couldn't believe—or refused to believe—what he was witnessing.

"There are two kinds of Russians in this world," Minotaur said. "Those who achieve the Center's goals, and those who die."

Rezident jerked open his desk drawer, probably to grab a pistol, but Minotaur aimed and pulled the trigger, hitting him in the neck. His head flopped forward, and he gurgled and gagged. He convulsed, and blood leaked onto his desk calendar and spread to his pen set and phone.

The young officer jumped from his seat and nearly fell over the back of his chair.

Bear swung out his shotgun and aimed at the young man, but Minotaur motioned for him to hold his fire.

"Who are you?" Minotaur asked.

"Me?" the young man asked.

The Rezident continued his noisy death throes.

"You see anyone else in the room?" Minotaur asked.

The younger man's voice was shaky: "I'm not important. I'm simply the Assistant Rezident." There was a pause. "Are you going to kill me, too?"

Minotaur looked him straight in the eye and smiled. "That depends. Can you get me four to five pellets of ricin and a compressed air gun disguised as a camera to shoot the ricin?"

"Yes."

"As soon as possible—fly it here from Moscow if you have to."

"Yes, right away, Minotaur."

Minotaur gestured for the Assistant Rezident to hurry off.

The Assistant Rezident hastened out the door.

Minotaur turned to Bear and said, "Tomorrow, we will do surveillance in Saint Peter's Square so we have a better idea of the layout, security, and avenues of escape. Next week, we should have the ricin and the camera. When Pope Francis gives his weekly speech, we'll administer the ricin."

Bear nodded in agreement.

"Are you sure the pope won't know he's been shot?" Bear asked.

"Georgi Markov didn't," Minotaur said, referring to the dissident writer assassinated in 1978 with a ricin shot from a delivery weapon disguised as an umbrella.

Bear smiled. "I'm looking forward to it."

"Likewise."

Chapter Twenty-Eight

Chris and Sonny met in the waiting room, hoping to hear that Max and Tom had survived the BK-16 virus. Chris braced himself for the worst—both of them dead—but he hoped for the best.

"Taking them long enough," Sonny said.

Chris looked at his watch—it was 5:13 PM. Times like this he'd rather be shot at than wait; at least he could do something about getting shot at.

A doctor arrived. She wasn't smiling. Chris straightened up, and Sonny directed his attention to her.

"Mr. Johnson?" the doctor called out.

Chris was disappointed not to be called but judging from the doctor's unhappy face, she had bad news, and it would be better to wait for the good news.

The doctor approached Chris and Sonny. "Mr. Johnson?"

Sonny thumped Chris on the thigh and said, "Dude."

Then Chris remembered his alias: *Johnson*. He stood. "Yes?"

The doctor took a breath. "Your friends are okay. Their vitals are improving rapidly. They're still in a weakened state, but if they improve at this rate, we should be able to release them tomorrow."

Chris was overwhelmed with relief. "Can we go see them?"

"Sure. Follow me, please." The doctor escorted Chris and Sonny through the halls and into one of the patient rooms. "I have some other patients to attend to," the doctor said as they walked in, "but the nurse will be here in a few minutes."

"Thank you," Chris said.

Sonny grunted.

Both Max and Tom were lying awake in their beds.

Seeing the two of them alive made Chris smile. Sonny smiled, too. It was contagious because Max and Tom grinned, too.

"Where's Angelo?" Max asked.

"He brought the boat here to Naples," Sonny said.

"He's waiting for us at the pier," Chris said.

Max used his arms to help him sit up. "You've got to break us out of here."

"Seriously?" Chris asked.

"I hate hospitals," Max replied.

Chris looked at Tom and waited to see if he had an opinion on the matter.

"Ditto," Tom said.

Sonny chuckled. "The hospital staff is going to be pissed."

"Hopefully we're out of here before then," Chris said. He picked up Max's civilian clothes and laid them next to him on the bed.

Max went commando, putting his pants on without undershorts. His movements were wobbly and sluggish.

Chris helped Max untie his gown, and Sonny assisted Tom, but even with their help, the going was sluggish, and the nurse was due to arrive any minute. Breaking out of the hospital seemed like a simple, trivial mission, but Chris's heart beat rapidly, and he felt the anxiousness of a schoolboy up to mischief.

Max and Tom finished dressing, but they were still shaky on their feet, so Chris and Sonny acted as their crutches. When they neared the door, Chris peeked outside to see if the coast was clear. A handful of people—visitors, patients, and nurses—milled about the hallway, but no nurses seemed headed in their direction. "Go," Chris said.

Instead of a high-speed getaway, Max and Tom made a low-speed hobble.

"Can't you move your ass?" Sonny asked.

"Going as fast as I can," Tom said. He ran out of breath trying to walk and talk at the same time.

It was like helping Forrest Gump escape the bullies in the truck, except that Gump was still in his cumbersome leg braces.

They exited the hospital and hopped in the car with Sonny and Max in front and Chris and Tom in back. Chris's heart continued to race until Sonny drove them out of the parking lot, and he could breathe easy.

"Hooah!" Sonny cheered.

The four of them basked in juvenile giddiness at the stunt they'd just pulled off.

It was still raining, and Max asked, "Where's the rest of the antidote?"

It was a happy topic. "CIA boys came up from Rome and picked it up," Chris said brightly. But it was related to a sad topic. "They took Hannah, too." His eyes watered, and the more he remembered, the more the tears built up. He didn't want Tom or anyone else to see him cry, but he didn't want to forget. Silently he looked out the side window and wept.

When they arrived at the pier, Chris dried his eyes.

Angelo met them on the stern of the muscle yacht. "Sonny told me about Hannah," he said. "I'm sorry."

"It's okay," Chris said. It wasn't okay. In fact, it was damn far from okay, but Chris didn't say that. Angelo was a good guy, and he had nothing to apologize for.

They sat together in the private area of the upper deck, cleaned their weapons, and topped off their ammo. Angelo broke out food, but Chris wasn't hungry. Still, he forced himself to eat, but his sense of smell and taste was dead.

Chris's phone rang. It was from Willy. Chris answered, "Hello?"

"I'm on the pier now," Willy said, "and I'm coming aboard. Don't nobody shoot me."

Chris told the others.

Willy came across the gangway, and Angelo rushed out to greet him. "Welcome aboard, sir. Please, have a seat."

Willy sat in the pilot's chair as if to assert his authority; at least, that's how it seemed to Chris.

"Hannah was one of the best," Willy said. "One of a kind. I'm going to miss her."

Max and Tom nodded in agreement, but Chris and Sonny continued to prep their weapons.

Willy turned to the brothers and asked, "How you boys feeling?"

"Better," Max said.

"Better and better," Tom said.

"Good," Willy said. He studied the four of them for a moment. Then he cut to the chase: "Crackerjack work. You accomplished the mission. Now I'm here to take you all home." He seemed to attempt some humor: "Except for you, Angelo; you're already home."

No one laughed; instead, there was an awkward silence.

"Why did Minotaur want the BK-16?" Max asked. "Who was it for?"

Willy seemed at a loss for words, but all eyes were on him and waiting. "Minotaur is a codename for one of Russia's top assassins. Langley believes he was assigned to use BK-16 to assassinate Pope Francis."

The four operators looked at each other incredulously, stunned by the significance of what they'd just heard. "What?" Max finally said.

"Moscow is upset about the pope's opposition to Russia trying to take over Ukraine," Willy said.

Seemingly out of the blue, Sonny asked, "Have you ever worked directly with Hannah?"

Willy seemed surprised by the sudden shift in topic. "Directly, this is the first mission we've had together. Indirectly, I've worked with her before."

Sonny grumbled: "I took my marching orders from her, not you. You're Max and Tom's buddy, not mine."

Chris agreed, but he didn't say it. "I want Minotaur."

"I understand how you feel," Willy said, "but getting Minotaur is not our mission."

"Have you asked Langley about going after Minotaur and his crew?" Max asked.

"I did," Willy said.

"What'd they say?" Tom asked.

"Nothing," Willy said. "Still waiting for an answer."

Chris persisted: "Minotaur is here in Rome now. If we're ever going to get him, now is the time."

Willy spoke patiently: "Rendering him is not our mission. At least not yet."

"I understand it's not your mission," Chris said. "You've made that clear." He looked around the table. "Who wants to get Minotaur—dead or alive?"

Thunder rumbled.

Willy leaned forward and returned fire. "Not with Company equipment—that means no weapons, no ammo, no comms, no fancy yacht—none of it." He looked at Angelo and added, "No assets or support personnel, either."

Angelo avoided eye contact with Willy.

Sonny glared at Willy and said, "You don't have to be an asshole about it."

Willy glared at Sonny. "I'm trying to deescalate this, and you're throwing gas on the fire."

"Hannah saved my life in that shootout with Minotaur's men," Max said.

Willy looked to Tom, as if soliciting his support.

"She helped us get the antidote and saved Max and me," Tom said.

Willy shook his head. "I can't have you four running vigilante around Italy and causing an international incident."

"It'll be an international incident if Pope Francis is assassinated," Chris said.

Willy rubbed the back of his head. "You know what I mean."

"How long do we have before we have to return to the States?" Max asked.

Willy raised his voice, and his pitch got higher, too: "This ain't open for discussion or debate. I'm telling you to get your asses on the plane and go home!"

"And we're telling you to screw yourself!" Sonny shouted.

Willy took it down a notch and used a careful, controlled tone: "Solomon Cohen, you've got a reputation in CIA as being difficult to work with. It was Hannah who took you off the blacklist. You don't want to be on that list again, and you sure as hell don't want to be on my list."

"Willy, you don't listen so well," Chris said. "It isn't only Sonny telling you to screw yourself. All four of us are telling you to screw yourself."

Willy bared his teeth, and his eyes protruded. "Christopher Paladin, when you left Team Six and became a preacher, the world forgot about you—except for Hannah. You're not a Tier One operator anymore. You're not even CIA. You're just a temp."

Max didn't seem the diplomatic type, but Willy was his buddy, and Max was patient with him. "Hannah was good to us; now it's time for us to be good to her."

"She wouldn't want this," Willy said. "Not like this."

Chris slammed his fist on the table with a mighty boom. "You don't know what she'd want!"

"An eye for an eye," Sonny said.

Willy looked at Tom as if hoping he wouldn't be part of this mutiny.

Tom shrugged his shoulders. "What they said."

Willy narrowed his eyes at Tom before he shook his head and stood. "This won't end well, boys. Mark my words, this won't end well." His eyes drifted off into that thousand-yard stare, and he stormed off the yacht without another word.

The sky rumbled again.

Chapter Twenty-Nine

U nder the cover of night, they sailed from Naples to the municipality of Rome and moored the yacht in the Ostia marina. That morning, Willy's words knifed Chris in the gut—*this won't end well*—but the next morning did begin well, with hot beverages and pastries, courtesy of Angelo. Chris was mad as hell, and his appetite returned.

Tom examined his smartphone. "Every Wednesday, Pope Francis addresses a general audience in Saint Peter's Square. Tomorrow is Wednesday."

Chris drank a hot cup of *caffè d'orzo*—an espresso-style roasted barley drink without caffeine. It tasted nutty. "If the pope shows up tomorrow, I'm sure Minotaur will, too, whether it be to do surveillance or the actual assassination."

"We should be there, too," Max said.

"Do we need tickets?" Chris asked.

Tom sipped a caffè d'orzo. "Yes, but they're free. Today we can pick some up at Saint Peter's Square."

"We better get tickets before they run out," Sonny said.

Max had a *caffè latte*. In Italy, if someone ordered a *latte*, all they got was milk; if they wanted espresso with their milk, they had to order caffè latte. "Whoever picks up the tickets will likely need to pass through security and x-ray machines without his *pistolet* and knife collection."

Sonny held his cup of espresso and stared at Tom. "We only need one person to pick up the tickets, don't we?"

The others stared at Tom, too.

Angelo stayed out of it, eating *strudel di mele*, apple strudel.

"What about Angelo?" Tom asked. "Can't he get the tickets?"

"He could," Chris said, "but we don't need anyone screwing with the boat while we're gone. And if we have to get out of Dodge fast, we may want Angelo already on the boat with the engine running."

Sonny stuffed his mouth with *cornetto*, a smaller, less buttery, lighter version of a croissant.

Tom seemed surprised that everyone had suddenly ganged up on him, but he was the youngest member of the group, and it was an un-written code that all the crap jobs went to the junior guy. "What if I run into Minotaur or one of his men while I'm getting tickets?"

"I'll be armed and standing nearby if you get in trouble," Sonny said. "Just outside of Vatican City. If you call for help, I'll hop the bar-ricade and come runnin'."

Tom surrendered quietly. "Okay." He nibbled on an apricot *crosta-ta*, an Italian tart.

Chris glanced at Max and then Tom. "You two sure you're up for this? You were flat on your backs yesterday."

Max grunted with a mouthful of crostata.

"We're at about seventy-five percent strength now," Tom said.

Chris had the crostata, too. "Super."

"We still don't know what Minotaur looks like," Sonny said, "and according to Willy, no Agency resources will be coming our way—that means no intel."

"We can work out some alternatives of who we're looking for," Chris said.

Max swallowed his crostata. "Slavic features."

"Could be wearing a disguise," Tom said.

"Everyone makes a tactical mistake," Max said. "And when Mino-taur does, we'll catch it."

"Unless he plays a perfect game," Sonny said.

There was an uncomfortable silence until Chris broke it: "I know we're desperate, and the odds are against us, but the stakes are high, and it's all we've got."

CHRIS, MAX, SONNY, and Tom finished breakfast, swiftly geared up, and drove from Ostia to just northwest of the Colosseum, where they crossed the Tiber River. They parked on the third floor of Terminal Gianicolo, a five-story parking garage and food court for tourists. Except for Sonny, they stashed their pistols in concealed compartments in the doors before they exited the vehicle—when they returned to the vehicle, they would rearm themselves.

The four men strolled through the garage and passed a trio of blazing Italian beauties. "Bada-bing, bada-boom," Max said within earshot of the team but out of earshot of the ladies.

"A lot of moustaches and not a lot of trimming," Sonny said.

"Have you been with an Italian woman?" Max asked.

"No," Sonny said.

Max rolled his eyes. "That says a lot."

Unusual for Sonny, he had no comeback.

They split up in pairs at the garage entrance—Max and Chris were one pair and Sonny and Tom were the other—so they wouldn't look conspicuous with all four of them together. Soon Chris and Max strolled past shops and *gelati* stands, pretending to be tourists. When they neared Vatican City, Chris eyed five light blue subcompact cars, each with the word *POLIZIA* written under a white stripe. Three of the Italian national police cars were parked east of Largo del Colonnato Street, the Italian side of the border, and two were parked to the west, on the Vatican side. Vatican City was the smallest country in the world, and its head of state was the pope.

Italian police officers on both sides of the border wore dark blue shirts and gray trousers. The policemen and their vehicles on the Vatican City side were there by a long-standing agreement between the two nations, but their authority extended only as far as the Vatican allowed.

Sonny remained on the Rome side of the border as Tom entered Vatican City to the right and passed through a security x-ray machine.

Meanwhile, Chris and Max were screened by security to the left before they entered Piazza San Pietro—Saint Peter's Square. Chris didn't know what Minotaur looked like, but he scanned the square for telltale signs of professional surveillance, such as someone with a preoccupation with videotaping security personnel—or someone focusing on tactical positions for hitting the pope. But he spotted no one out of the ordinary. An expert such as Minotaur would make his operational behavior appear natural. Finding him seemed impossible, and Chris was frustrated.

Entering Vatican City, Chris continued to blend in with the other tourists. In the center of Saint Peter's Square, bronze lions hefted a red granite obelisk, a sun dial that towered over a hundred feet tall. Chris used his smartphone to take pictures of Max in front of it.

Two water fountains flanked the obelisk, and to the outside of them stood four rows of columns in half circles. Above the columns rested more than a hundred statues of religious figures. The whole plaza was laid out in smiting symmetry. Chris took more pictures. The photos helped his cover as a tourist and created a reconnaissance record that he and his crew could study later.

"Do the fountains work?" Max asked.

"Vatican turn off because of drought," a stout woman said with an Italian accent.

Max nodded.

Chris and Max strolled over cobblestones and travertine. A Vatican City police officer in his black trousers and white shirt helped a tourist. Chris and Max passed a couple of nuns and others and approached Saint Peter's Basilica, towering at four hundred and forty-eight feet. Statues of Jesus Christ and his apostles adorned the top of the façade in front of the basilica's dome.

A clean-shaven man jabbered on his cell phone and, without seeming to pay attention to the people around him, backed into Chris. He grabbed Chris's arm, and his leg tangled with Chris's, almost knocking him off balance.

Chris twisted his arm away from the man on the phone and backed away from him, creating immediate distance. Max turned and gave Cell Phone the evil eye.

Meanwhile, someone else bumped into Chris from behind, but it didn't stop there—his hand fished into Chris's front pocket, where his wallet was stashed. Either this was a pickpocket or someone worse.

Chris grabbed the pickpocket's hand, pulled it out of his pocket, firmly pressed the base of his thumb knuckle at an angle, turned toward the thief, and caught a glimpse of his moustache before twisting his hand into a wristlock. Chris continued to twist and turn until Thief faced away from him. With one hand still holding Thief in a wristlock, Chris used his other hand to push the man's elbow at an angle.

Now Thief had a choice. He could stand his ground and end up with a broken wrist and elbow, or he could go with the flow of Chris's twisting and turning and kiss the cobblestones. Thief chose the latter and gave the concrete a smack. A pair of wallets and a purse spilled onto the ground beside him.

A woman pointed at the purse and shouted in fluent English, "That's my purse!"

His forehead bleeding, Thief struggled to his feet, left the wallets and purse, and staggered away. Cell Phone, who was probably an accomplice to distract Chris, maintained his composure and walked away, still on his phone.

The woman who'd told Max about the drought chased after Thief, pointing at him. "He stole my purse!"

The police officer stopped helping the tourist trio and chased after Thief, who took flight. Meanwhile, Cell Phone continued his leisurely pace.

Chris took photos of Thief and Cell Phone.

Max pointed to the top of the building to the right of Saint Peter's Square and Basilica. "On Sundays, the pope speaks from his apartment there. It'd take a sniper rifle to reach him, but that'd be a bulky weapon to sneak in and out of here, and firing it would make some noise."

Chris took another photo. "If Minotaur were using BK-16, I'd expect him to engage the pope up close and personal. But we took his BK-16 and destroyed the lab."

"He might still try for up close and personal," Max said.

"Tomorrow or the next Wednesday," Chris added.

"I'd guess sooner rather than later. And we'll be here, ready." Max took out his phone and examined the screen. A look of surprise crossed his face.

"What is it?" Chris asked.

Max's look of surprise transformed into a smile. "A license to kill."

"Willy?"

"He says kill or capture Minotaur—it's official. He's sent a physical description and photos."

Chris was elated. "Now we know who we're hunting."

"Tomorrow's security will be locked and loaded," Max said. "Won't be able to take in weapons."

"Two of us can go in unarmed, and two of us can stand nearby with concealed weapons as a quick reactionary force."

Max nodded. "Tom and I are used to working together, and you and Sonny have experience with each other, too—those will be the best pairings."

Chris nodded. "Tomorrow, we'll kill Minotaur."

Chapter Thirty

Early Wednesday morning, Max and the others drove into the heart of Rome. After parking, Chris and Sonny hid their weapons in the door compartments, while Max and Tom retained theirs. They exited the vehicle and went on foot to Vatican City. Max could feel his breath speeding up on him, so he took deep breaths to decelerate it.

Max and his brother remained on the Rome side of the border, their Glock pistols concealed under their clothing. They pretended to be interested in souvenirs, but they kept careful watch of their surroundings.

Security was tighter now, and Chris and Sonny lined up to pass through security and into Vatican City. Waves of people filled the boulevard, and soon the waves washed over the two men, hiding them from Max's view. He scanned for Minotaur but couldn't spot him.

For two and a half hours the line of visitors moved slowly, advancing into Vatican City. More than twenty thousand people poured into the square, and security stopped allowing people in.

From the Rome side, Max could see a pair of jumbotrons that broadcast live video of a priest reading out names of groups in attendance for today's event. The list seemed to go on ad nauseam.

Then Pope Francis rode into St. Peter's Square on his Popemobile. A children's choir sang "Ave Maria," and an ecstatic crowd drowned out their little voices.

Max continued to fake interest in souvenirs at a nearby stand when a physically fit man caught his eye. Other people were happy and excited, but this guy wasn't joining in the lovefest. Max looked for signs of a concealed weapon printing its shape in his clothing but couldn't spot one. Max watched his hands to see if they reached for a weapon. "See the grumpy athletic guy with the mushroom hairstyle loitering near the gelati stand?" he whispered.

Tom pretended to examine keychains with pictures of the pope. "Hang on." He shifted his attention to keychains with Saint Peter's Basilica on them. "Yeah, I think so."

"What's he doing there?"

"Doesn't seem interested in the gelati," Tom said. "What about the well-built guy in the red shirt—standing near him?"

"Are they together?"

"Don't know."

Mushroom spoke with Red.

Max answered his own question: "Looks like they are."

Red glanced down at his own hip as if he was concerned whether or not his concealed weapon was showing.

A young *carabinieri* approached Red. The carabinieri wore confidence and alertness with his camouflage uniform and navy blue beret. He was part of a military police unit that had civilian authority, the national gendarmerie of Italy, roughly similar to the FBI in the US. Max wondered if he, too, had picked up on the significance of Red's glance. Sometimes Max could pinpoint what didn't fit, but other times he only felt it, and he didn't know why.

Mushroom and Red turned away from the young carabinieri and Saint Peter's Square. They hustled along the cobblestone road that was Via della Conciliazione, closed to public vehicles but not pedestrians.

The young carabinieri picked up his pace and followed.

Tom stepped away from the souvenir stand. "That carabinieri is going to need help."

All hell was about to break loose, and Max's breaths became shorter and fleeting. "We don't know where Minotaur is yet."

Tom walked in the carabinieri's direction. "The carabinieri needs our help," he repeated.

Max followed. Tom sped up. Max did, too.

The carabinieri called out to Mushroom and Red in Italian. He didn't wait for a response before he called out in English: "Just a minute, I want to talk with you."

Mushroom and Red ignored him and kept going.

"Stop, police!" the carabinieri called out in English.

Some bystanders avoided the policeman, giving him a wide berth. Others stopped and rubbernecked. A pair of twenty-somethings whipped out their phones and filmed the action, probably to post to their social media accounts.

Mushroom and Red dashed away and ducked into a small street to the left. The carabinieri turned the corner after them.

Shit.

Max and Tom sprinted around the corner. Two four-story buildings shaded the narrow cobblestone street, which was only wide enough for one car, but a barricade prevented vehicles from entering. Instead, about three dozen people occupied the alley; some looked lost, some shopped, some walked, and some were sitting down. Mushroom and Red stopped, spun around, and blasted Beretta 9mm pistols at the carabinieri.

Pedestrians screamed, scattered, collapsed, and froze. One round struck Max in the shoulder like someone had stabbed him with a hot knife. The carabinieri returned fire with a Beretta and took down Red, but the officer went down, too. Then Mushroom moved in as if about to finish off the carabinieri.

Max drew his pistol, and Tom did, too, but Tom was in Max's line of fire, and he couldn't shoot Mushroom without shooting Tom. Max took a step to the side.

Pop, pop, pop! Tom shot Mushroom, and he fell.

Boom! The sound came from behind Max. He felt as if he'd been struck in the back by a car, but he thought the place had been barricaded from vehicles entering. Max did a belly-flop on the street. He couldn't breathe. He couldn't get up. He didn't know if he was stunned, paralyzed, or dying. The warmth of oozing blood spread across his back, and his vision of the cobblestones beneath him blurred and shrank. Someone with heavy footsteps passed him from behind and pumped a shotgun.

"Max!" Tom yelled before he got off a shot: *Pop!*

Max could hear, and he strained his neck up to see.

Boom!

Tom's chest erupted in blood, and he landed on his back. A monstrous man armed with a sawed-off shotgun spit tobacco juice. He closed in and aimed at Tom's head.

Tommy! Max's pistol was in his hand, and he pointed it at the center of the monstrous man's head and pulled the trigger. A chunk of the top of the monster's head and a burst of blood flew through the air. He toppled over like a stone statue.

Max crawled to his brother. "Ungh." His life light was fading fast. He knew he wouldn't survive a trip to Naples and therefore needed a nearby hospital, but he didn't want civilian doctors and nurses to discover his weapon and alert the police. He was too weak now to use it, anyway. He looked for a sewer to ditch it in, but he didn't spot one. He reached the fallen monster and slipped his pistol underneath him. Then Max stripped off his belt and ammo and stuck it under the man, too. He didn't have the energy to wipe the fingerprints.

People cried and shouted, and sirens blared. Someone took pictures. The narrow street was chaotic. Max was dying, but his mind became consumed with his brother's safety. He reached Tom, who'd crawled to the carabinieri and deposited his gun and other kit with the motionless soldier. His younger brother was like him, and it made his heart proud.

Max wheezed. "The Canadian Embassy is three hundred meters from here."

Tom was a bloody mess, and his breathing was labored: "I can't make it three hundred meters."

"You don't look bad," Max lied.

Police rushed into the alley yelling in Italian. People shouted in Italian, English, French, and other languages. It was pandemonium.

Tom was right—neither of them could make it to the Canadian Embassy. But Max didn't want to be arrested, either. Max and Tom crawled to the side of the street and collapsed. They couldn't crawl anymore.

A young woman sat next to them in tears. "It all happened so fast," she cried in French.

The color bled out of the world, and the edges of Max's vision darkened. The circle of light shrank tighter and tighter. Pretending he was a civilian, he asked her in French, "Are you okay?"

She looked at him with the face of his deceased mother. She was so young. "*Oui*," she said.

"I thought they were going to kill us," Max said, before turning to check on his brother.

Tom closed his eyes and sank to the pavement.

Max wanted to say, *Stay with me, Tommy*. But he didn't know if the words came out of his mouth. His vision became a pinhole, and it was too taxing to try and see anymore. Then all went black.

"Rest, honey," his mother's voice said.

Chapter Thirty-One

Wednesday morning dawned cool, but Chris burned with a fever to kill. In Terminal Gianicolo, he paired up with Sonny, and Max took Tom as his buddy. When they reached the border, Max and Tom stayed on the Rome side, and Chris and Sonny queued up to enter Vatican City. Chris glanced at his watch: 6:47 a.m.

At the front of the line stood eight carabinieri. Chris hadn't seen them yesterday, and he wondered if this was standard for Wednesday morning, or if it was something new. The line grew and grew, but the carabinieri weren't letting visitors pass. Ironically, some people tried to cut in line to attend this holy event, but other visitors yelled at them in gesturing Italian, multiple varieties of English, and a Slavic language. The cheaters retreated.

For the next two and a half hours of waiting in line, Chris thought of finding Minotaur and killing him—roundhouse punch to the temple, snapping his neck, or a vicious curb stomp. He scanned the area for Minotaur or his men but couldn't ID them. The crowd was so thick that when he looked back, he couldn't even see Max or Tom.

At 8:29, a carabinieri started checking tickets, two others examined bags, and another waved his handheld metal detector over people. The line advanced slowly. An Asian family didn't have tickets, and a carabinieri waved them away, denying them admission.

Chris took his turn in line and showed his ticket. The carabinieri studied it and waved him through the first checkpoint. A carabinieri with a thin Spanish-style beard turned away a white couple who had tickets but were underdressed in their shorts and tank tops.

"Dumbasses," Sonny muttered.

Admitted were ticket-toting visitors who wore conservative clothing that didn't expose their skin: men in pants and short-sleeved shirts and women in pants, capris, dresses and skirts covering their knees, and short-sleeved blouses. Chris and Sonny were dressed appropriately, too, wearing tan slacks and polo shirts. Even so, the tension of the undecided fueled his fever. *Will we make it through?* Because he didn't have a bag, he was swept with the wand and expeditiously admitted—so was Sonny.

The race was on. A red-haired priest, two laughing nuns, a group of people wearing matching yellow T-shirts, and a slew of others dashed past thousands of chairs lined in rows to get to the front seats in St. Peter's Square. Chris and Sonny jogged to chairs in an aisle near the center, giving them a tactical view of the square, basilica, and jumbotrons.

The square rapidly filled to over twenty thousand people, and a priest moseyed over to the microphone at the top of the steps in front of the basilica and began reading names of groups attending. The atmosphere was festive, but Chris wasn't smiling. Neither was Sonny, which was often his nature, and there was no changing that. Two grumpy men in good physical shape were sure to set off the spider senses of the pope's security team. Even if Vatican City security personnel didn't notice them, Minotaur or one of his clan might. Chris tried to lose his frown, but he was still angry and bitter over Hannah's death, and there was no faking it.

He tried to remember something positive. In Washington, DC, he'd floated in a white swan boat with Hannah on the Tidal Basin, and white cherry blossoms glided through the air. Their beauty was silken and vibrant, without regret. Down came the petals—warriors falling in battle—magnificent and glorious. Like soldiers, the cherry blossoms came and went with the fleetingness of dreams. Like Hannah. They lived as they died and died as they lived. The blossoms covered Potomac Park as if they were white markers in the field of Arlington Cemetery. Such markers might fade, but the sacrifices lived on. Chris still couldn't smile, but some of the burden on his heart lifted, and his frown dissolved.

Dressed in Renaissance uniforms of Medici blue, red, and yellow, the Pontifical Swiss Guard, Vatican City's military, spread out at regular intervals around the barricaded-in crowd. The Guard's duty was to protect the pope and the Apostolic Palace. Adding extra security were the Vatican City Police. Chris knew the square was likely swarming with plainclothes officers, too.

Pope Francis rolled into the square on his Popemobile, a white Ford Focus with the windows rolled down. Twenty Swiss Guards dressed in modern black suits jogged alongside or rode with him, similar to the way the US Secret Service accompanied the presidential limousine. People waved, cheered, and called out *"Viva il Papa!"* Pope Francis smiled and waved back at them. A rainbow of flags from different countries rippled in a breeze, and thousands of tourists and pilgrims snapped photos with their smartphones and cameras. The flashes sparkled like stars in the sky.

The Popemobile stopped near Chris's section, and one of the bodyguards brought the pope a baby from the crowd. He kissed it, and the bodyguard returned the child to its mother. A woman cried out hysterically, and the Popemobile moved on. Soon it stopped again. Pope Francis signed a young boy's handmade poster and greeted a pair of Buddhist monks before kissing more babies.

The air electrified. Angelo had told Chris earlier: "People came to hear Pope Benedict; now they come to touch Francis."

Chris couldn't fully experience the joy in the air, but it softened his heart, and he was suddenly surprised to find his feelings of hatred and anger mellowing. He hadn't realized how the emotions had darkened him—until now, when sunlight touched his soul. He couldn't forgive Minotaur, but in a slice of time, his thirst for revenge left him. He knew right then that he wanted to stay a minister of the Lord.

Even so, his focus snapped back to his surroundings. He wanted to finish his job as a covert operator. If anyone could walk a tightrope between being a minister and an operator, Chris knew it was him. Dead or alive: that was his mission.

A children's choir sang, "Amazing grace, how sweet the sound that saved a wretch like me. I once was lost, but now am found, was blind but now I see..." Chris thought of it as a Protestant hymn, and he was surprised to hear it here in Saint Peter's Square. The music warmed him and made him feel at home. It was as if God had sent him a text message: I love you. The burden on Chris's shoulders lifted.

The pope rode around another section. Men, women and children stood on seats to see him, blocking Chris's direct line of sight.

Sonny clenched Chris's shoulder and pointed. "There."

The jumbotron showed a live video of the pope, who'd stopped near a group where a gray-haired man in a gray suit stood taking pictures with his smartphone. It was the man in the photos Willy had sent—Minotaur. Beside him was an Italian who looked like a young Al Pacino—one of the men from the shootout that killed Hannah. Chris wanted to bag and drag them, but they were twenty meters away—in another section. The Swiss Guards and Vatican Police between Minotaur's section and Chris's didn't seem like they'd let people jump sections.

Chris tried to come up with a plausible ruse. He could tell the Swiss Guard that his and Sonny's wives were in the other section and they wanted to join them, but it was a lame excuse, and he struggled to think of a better one.

Because most of the visitors in Saint Peter's Square stood on their seats or abandoned them to get close to the barricades, it gave Chris space to maneuver within his own section. "Let's go."

Chris and Sonny swam through the crowd in the direction of Minotaur. He must've sensed them because he turned around and locked eyes with Chris. "I've got you," Chris thought. Minotaur seemed surprised that he'd been made. Then his surprise turned to contempt.

The Russian melted in the opposite direction, and Al Pacino went with him.

Chris advanced to the barricades at the end of his section, but he couldn't cross them without drawing the unwanted attention of security. Minotaur and Pacino continued to move to the edge of their own section, increasing the gap between them and Chris and Sonny. Chris leaned over the barricade and told a tall Swiss Guard, "I saw a man with a gun."

"What?" the Guard asked in English.

"We saw a man with a gun," Sonny said.

A woman overheard them and gasped.

"Where?" the Guard asked.

Max and Sonny pointed in Minotaur's direction. "In the front left section facing the basilica."

The gasping woman chattered something in Italian to the man next to her and pointed in the same direction. Others craned their heads toward Minotaur and Pacino.

A nearby Vatican cop gestured at the Guard, *What?*

Tall Guard rapidly chattered something in Italian into his mic, then turned to Chris and Sonny and said, "Take me."

Minotaur and Pacino slipped through the crowd, away from the basilica.

Chris and Sonny bounded over the barricade, crossed over the path where the Popemobile had ridden earlier, and led Tall Guard over the next barricades and into Minotaur and Pacino's section. Police stirred in the vicinity, possibly in response to Tall Guard's radio transmission.

Gunshots and screams rang out from the back of the square, where Max and Tom were positioned.

Chris glanced at a jumbotron, which cut away from the Popemobile and the Pope's security detail hauling booty out of the square.

Tall Guard split off in the direction of the sound of gunshots, but Chris shoved through the crowd toward Minotaur and Pacino, who now abandoned all attempts at stealth and hopped over the barriers of their section.

A Vatican police officer and Swiss Guard shouted at them, but Minotaur and Pacino were too speedy. Then a curly-haired man balancing a child in each arm and a woman carrying a baby climbed over the barricades; they were soon followed by a throng of panicked people. The floodgates had opened. Vatican police and Swiss Guards shouted orders and pushed back, but they were overwhelmed. The anxious chatter of frightened civilians rose to a roar and barricades toppled. More Vatican cops and Swiss Guards rushed to stop them, but the dam had broken, and there was no putting the water back in.

Chris lost sight of Minotaur and Pacino in the masses. He thought that if he pressed farther he'd spot them, but the density of the crowd was restricting his movement. He climbed up on the reservoir rim of a fountain for a greater view.

A Vatican City policeman chased Minotaur and Pacino through the south colonnade.

Chris hopped off the fountain, plowed through a group of men, and landed two columns deep in the colonnade. The Vatican City policeman reached the end of his jurisdiction, the border between Vatican City and Rome, and paused. Chris and Sonny raced past him and into Rome.

"*Arresto!*" the Vatican police officer called out from behind.

Chris and Sonny chased Minotaur and Pacino across the street and up a steep flight of steps between two buildings. Near the top of the stairs, Chris's thighs burned, but he kept pumping. He cleared the top and rushed through an iron gate. *Have I lost them?* He turned a corner and spotted the doors to an old ornate church. *Maybe that's them.* With Sonny breathing hard next to him, he sprinted up more steps, threw open the doors, and burst inside.

The doors of the church closed, but instead of the hushed, muffled reverence he'd normally expect, there was a disturbance, like ripples on a quiet pond. *I'm on the right trail.* Paintings of religious figures adorned the small, narrow chapel, and an elderly Caucasian couple sat on a pew leaning away from the center aisle. A priest called out to Minotaur and Pacino in a mixture of Italian and Dutch, but the two escaped through the back.

Chris and Sonny kept the heat on and blew out the back door of the church and ran across a shadowy walkway. One story below them was an aged sidewalk, and one story above and to the right stood a row of trees. To the left were the backs of a row of two-story buildings. Chris ran as hard as he could. They didn't seem to be gaining on Minotaur and Pacino, but he wasn't about to give up.

He pursued them up an incline. His leg muscles tightened, and he formed his lips into a circle and shot big breaths of oxygen straight to his lungs to get more air. Sonny was right with him.

Minotaur and Pacino stopped in front of a wall.

To their right, someone called out "*Policia!*" and some other words in Italian.

Pacino vaulted over the wall, but Minotaur was slower to clear the obstacle.

A policeman came into view and bounded over the wall after the fugitives.

Not knowing what they were all jumping into, Chris hesitated, but Sonny kept his pace and beat him over the wall.

Chris took a deep breath and vaulted, but when he saw what was on the other side, he grasped the top of the wall and held on. It was a two-story drop!

Pacino was off kilter as he staggered to his feet on the sidewalk below.

Minotaur must've landed like a cat, because he dashed away without signs of injury.

The police officer lay on his stomach with part of a broken femur busting through the back leg of his trousers. "Aieee!"

Sonny had landed one story below on a ledge before losing his perch and falling down another story. He landed on Pacino, pressing the man to the ground under him. Both men went limp.

Chris lost his grip and dropped, but he landed on the ledge a story below. Then he fell again. He righted himself in flight, and when he hit ground, his legs buckled and he tumbled. He bruised his hip and dirtied his shirt and trousers, but he was okay. He eyed the police officer's Beretta Model 92 FS pistol. Chris rushed over to him and took it. "*Grazie.*"

The policeman shouted something at him.

Chris locked and loaded a round in the chamber and concealed the barrel of the Beretta in his pocket. The handle stuck out, but he gripped it with his hand, concealing much of it.

From the heap on the ground, Sonny recovered first and zip-tied Pacino's hands behind his back.

"I got this sonofabitch!" Sonny shouted. "You get the other one!" His words motivated Chris to charge harder.

Minotaur sprinted through traffic and over a bridge. Below the bridge flowed the shallow, yellowish water of the Tiber River.

Chris burned in hot pursuit.

Police sirens pierced the air, converging on Vatican City. As Chris reached the bridge, a flashing siren on a squad car approached. Both Chris and Minotaur stopped running and walked, camouflaging themselves with the civilians. Chris realized he was holding his breath, so he breathed deep and long. The police car sped by.

Minotaur resumed flight. He passed high-rises and crossed a street before he ducked into the back of a building. Chris rushed into the building, too, and discovered a bohemian boutique with a handsome young shopkeeper and no customers. The front door swung shut, but Minotaur wasn't in sight. The shopkeeper greeted Chris, but he sped past the man and burst out the front door.

Minotaur turned a corner.

Chris pursued him several blocks before losing him at an intersection. He could've escaped via any combination of side streets and buildings, and Chris had no idea where he was.

A painter sat on a folding chair on the sidewalk and texted on his smartphone. Beside him were displayed a collection of paintings. Behind him was the buff façade of a 1930s apartment building. On it read a plaque: *PIAZZA DI TOR SANGUIGNA.*

Chris made a gesture of running and asked the painter, "Where is he?"

The painter froze.

Chris worried that the painter might've noticed the pistol handle sticking out of his pocket, but there wasn't much he could do about it. He pulled out a handful of euros and held them out. "Where is he?" Chris made a running gesture.

The artist pointed to an arcade in the apartment building. "*Là.*"

Chris pointed to the same spot to confirm. "There?"

"*Sì.*"

Chris gave him the money.

The artist smiled.

Chris inspected the arcade. Inside, twenty feet below, was a subterranean level on which stood a massive ancient arch that opened up to a stadium. The top of the arch was at eye level.

"*Circus Agonalis,*" the artist said.

Circus Maximus was the Colosseum, so Chris guessed that Circus Agonalis was the name of this smaller stadium. The Colosseum could seat around sixty-five thousand spectators, but this stadium looked like it only held about twenty thousand. Even so, the arena of this stadium was the length of two or more football fields.

Chris squinted to see Minotaur below, but the area was vast and had plenteous shadows. He had to get to Minotaur before the Russian found an exit. Chris climbed over the railing and did a dead hang to shave off some of the twenty-foot drop before he fell the remaining fourteen feet.

He bent his knees a little and tucked in his elbows and chin, preparing to do a parachute landing fall. His feet hit the hard ground, and he buckled. Immediately he rolled sideways on the balls of his feet. Distributing the impact so he wouldn't break his legs, he struck the side of his calf first, thigh next, hip, and finally the side of his back. His hip stung from where he'd bumped it before.

Chris was staggering to his feet when a shadow lunged at him. He attempted to roll out of the shadow's line of attack, but it caught him in the nose with a mighty crack. Both Chris and the shadow landed on the ground. They rose to their feet, but Chris had a pistol in his hand now. Drawing and aiming it was an automatic response that he didn't have to think about. Now Minotaur was in his sights.

Minotaur raised his hands in surrender and breathed hard. Even so, he managed a smile and puffed up his chest proudly. His eyes locked on Chris's, and his tone was arrogant. "In this cosmic lie we call the universe, we create our own values, and then we meet the monster."

Blood oozed from Chris's nose. "Death is no monster, and the righteous need not fear it. But you should be afraid. You should be very afraid."

"Mmm, but I'm not. If you were going to shoot me, you would've already done so."

Chris paused. Then he lowered his weapon.

Minotaur's smile broadened. "You Westerners are naïve. You like to play fair. If I were armed and threatening you, you could kill me, but you can't shoot me like this, an unarmed man. You will capture me. Then my people will make a deal. And I'll be back."

A serenity filled Chris. The anger was gone. And so was the pain. The loneliness didn't sting as much, and in its place, he had hope for a brighter tomorrow. "I just have one question."

"What is that?" Minotaur asked.

Chris studied the man for what seemed like a full minute. "Have you ever seen a cherry blossom?"

The smile on Minotaur's lips twisted like a pair of question marks. "No—why?"

Chris pointed the Beretta and squeezed the trigger. *Bang!* A scarlet hole dotted Minotaur between his gray eyes, and chunks of gray brain matter and white skull flew out the back in a mist of blood. His body collapsed under its own weight and landed in a pile on the dirt of the ancient grounds. Chris was the lone spectator in the dimly lit stadium to view Minotaur's finale.

Epilogue

A *week later...*
Max bowed his head as he sat in his wheelchair on the lawn of Landstuhl Regional Medical Center in Germany. He looked up. "My last memory was Tom saying, 'I can't make it three hundred meters.'"

Sonny stood in front of him. "The Italian police said that Minotaur and his men attempted to assassinate Pope Francis, but they don't know Minotaur's name or who he's working for. And the police are searching for us. They don't know who we are or who we work for, either." Sonny proudly added, "Some in the Italian media are calling us angels. Langley says that the Italian police investigation is simply for show."

"Is the pope okay?" Max asked.

"Yes. He voiced his appreciation for his security and the law enforcement officers, especially the young carabinieri who sacrificed his life." Sonny's arms hung down over his crutches. "Sorry I wasn't there to help you and your brother."

Max held out his hand as if to stop Sonny from saying any more. "Don't. We got Minotaur. That was our mission."

The warmth of the sunshine felt good, and Max lifted his face to it. A gentle breeze soothed his skin.

Willy exited the hospital building. He pushed a wheelchair. He stopped on the lawn next to Max and Sonny.

Tom sat in the wheelchair. "Where's Chris?" he asked.

"He was here for a day and a half," Sonny said. "Probably got tired of watching you two numb nuts lying around in comas. The pair of you would still be in Rome if Chris and I hadn't broken you out of that civilian hospital."

Willy cleared his throat. "And out of the country. I might've had something to do with that."

"The only reason I'm still here is on account of getting to know little Nurse Müller," Sonny said.

"Thanks," Tom said. "I think we make a great team."

Sonny saluted with his middle finger.

Max and Tom returned the salute.

The salutes were a manly way of expressing intense affection and true friendship.

"This is a topnotch crew," Willy said.

"We'd be even better with Hannah," Max said.

The others nodded in agreement.

"You think Chris will be back?" Tom asked. "Seems like he only did this job for her."

"He was true to her in life, and he'll be true to her in death," Sonny said. "She'd want us to carry on with this work—even if it means carrying on without her."

Max looked Sonny in the eyes, then Tom. "We will."

GET A FREE BESTSELLER

To get your free copy of a bestseller, just visit my website here:
http://www.stephentemplin.com

ENJOY THIS BOOK?

If you enjoyed this book, I'd be grateful if you could spend just a few minutes to leave a review (it can be as short as you like) on the book's Amazon page. A review is a powerful way to bring my work to the attention of other readers.

Thank you,

Steve

ABOUT THE AUTHOR

S TEPHEN TEMPLIN is a *New York Times* and international best-selling author, with the movie rights to one of his books purchased by Vin Diesel. His books have been translated into thirteen languages. He publishes with three of the Big Five publishers: Simon & Schuster, Macmillan, and Hachette UK.

He wasn't a SEAL, but he completed Hell Week, qualified as a pistol and rifle expert, blew things up, and practiced small unit tactics during Basic Underwater Demolition/SEAL training. Then for fourteen years he lectured as a tenured professor at Meio University in Japan, where he also trained in the martial art aikido. His PhD is in education, and he lives in the Dallas-Fort Worth area. Secretly, he's a dark chocolate thief.

To connect with Steve and for updates about new releases, visit his website at http://www.stephentemplin.com.

ACKNOWLEDGMENTS

S EAL sniper veteran Kyle Defoor trained me in pistol and assault rifle to help my preparation for writing this series. In Afghanistan, Kyle was part of Operation Anaconda, where he fought in the Battle of Takur Ghar and was awarded a Bronze Star for valor.

Former Delta Force operator Larry Vickers instructed me in handgun and assault rifle shooting, as well. He served in many classified operations, including in Panama, Iraq, Somalia, and Bosnia. Most notable among these operations was the rescue of CIA agent Kurt Muse from imprisonment by forces under the command of dictator Manuel Noriega.

SEAL Team Six veteran John Koenig taught me marksmanship, demolitions, and small-unit tactics during the land warfare phase of Basic Underwater Demolition/SEAL training. Commander Koenig served in classified operations in Vietnam, as a MILGRU advisor in El Salvador, and a SEAL Team Six operator in Grenada and Panama. In Grenada, his team rescued Governor General Paul Scoon's family from house arrest. Commander Koenig's leadership and instruction were straightforward, his dark sense of humor brought high points during many long hours of training, and his experiences were invaluable. I will always be grateful.

While I lived in Japan, aikido seventh- and fourth-degree black belt masters Kabayama Sensei and Yamaguchi Sensei trained me in aikido. *Arigatou gozaimasu.*

Finally, I'd like to thank Jon Ford and Carol Scarr for their excellent editing.

This is a work of fiction. Any references to names, characters, organizations, places, events, and incidents are either products of the author's imagination or are used fictitiously. Some tactics have been changed to protect operators and their missions.

———— ◉ ————

All Rights Reserved © 2018 by Stephen Templin
No part of this book may be reproduced or transmitted in any form or by any means, graphic, electronic, or mechanical, including photocopying, recording, taping, or by any information storage or retrieval system, without the written permission of the publisher.

Published by Stephen Templin
http://www.stephentemplin.com
ISBN-13: 9781980244530
Cover design by Nuno Moreira

23615509R00120

Made in the USA
Columbia, SC
10 August 2018